DREAM WATER

DREAM WATER

KAREN RIVERS

ORCA BOOK PUBLISHERS

Canadian Cataloguing in Publication Data
Rivers, Karen, 1970–
Dream water

ISBN 1-55143-160-2 (bound). – ISBN 1-55143-162-9 (pbk)

I. Title.
PS8585.I8778D7 1999 jC813'.54 C99-910864-6
PZ7.R5224Dr 1999

Library of Congress Catalog Card Number: 99-65170

Orca Book Publishers gratefully acknowledges the support of our publishing programs provided by the following agencies: the Department of Canadian Heritage, The Canada Council for the Arts, and the British Columbia Arts Council.
Canadä

Cover design by Jim Brennan
Cover photographs: *whale* - Alexandra Morton; *models* - Jim Brennan: *author photo* - Tim Derkitt

Printed and bound in Canada

IN CANADA:	IN THE UNITED STATES:
Orca Book Publishers	Orca Book Publishers
PO Box 5626, Station B	PO Box 468
Victoria, BC Canada	Custer, WA USA
V8R 6S4	98240-0468

01 00 99 5 4 3 2 1

In memory of all those killed or injured by captive animals who have been robbed of their right to be free.

For my sisters, who understand the "whale dreams,"

and

for my parents, who gave me the opportunities to appreciate the beauty, power and freedom of orcas in the wild.

PROLOGUE

The day is not bright and the clouds drag low over the Pacific.

The ocean is not quiet, but alive with sounds. If you listen closely, you can hear the high calls of the orcas, the slap of water under their tails, the synchronized expulsion of air from their blowholes. They circle tightly around the frantic seals and trap their hunt against the rocky reef, feasting on the slippery pinnipeds that can't escape. The water churns. Through the foam and bubbles, they are visible as black-and-white shadows in the emerald green water. They whistle and click, and their sounds peal loudly across the ocean surface, resonating richly along the ocean floor.

If you could only hear over the sound of the city traffic and human noise, you would hear that.

They are only a few miles away; sounds are amplified over water.

Inside the Seaquarium, there is always a hum of voices and applause; the sea lions bark and the loudspeaker crackles as the next show is announced. Today there is the noisy chorus of children as well. It is cold, and they are tired and wet and overexcited by the sight of the three giant whales in the tiny pool. They jostle and shove and whisper and bang on the glass with mittened fists. They nudge each other and shriek as the huge mammals swim by.

But when the girl falls into the water, all the children stop talking.

Of course, it must be slippery. But aren't her boots designed with tiny, rippling grooves on the rubber soles to grip the dock's aqua blue surface?

She had been walking along the curving stage that looked, to the children, as though it was made of papier maché. The whale show was over, and on the upper decks of the Seaquarium the scanty crowd was moving on to see the sea lions taking a shower, or maybe the seals clapping their fins in salty applause. The children have already seen the whale show from above; they have been splashed and sprayed – squealing with delight and shock when the cold water doused them. Now, most of them are clustered around the windows below, having just watched the show again from the glass-windowed bottom where it's dry and safe. They have watched the giant black-and-white mammals spinning around the tiny pool, flying in and out in a wash of white spray.

The children are only interested in the whales. Not the seals or sea lions or exotic fish or even the giant octopus. The whales are the star attraction.

Where is the teacher? She must be over near the seal hospital, craning her neck to see the baby seals cradled in the arms of the keepers. She is probably asking him questions in her low melodious voice that all the boys are in love with, the girls in awe of. She has just turned away for a moment. So much can happen in the blink of an eye.

It is February. Inside the dark tunnels under the Seaquarium, the children are warm and protected. Outside the air is cold, with a sharp bite that draws a flush to their cheeks. The water must be very cold; it must have made the girl gasp. For a moment, it must have paralyzed her limbs, frozen her in place.

The crowd is small, of course – February in Canada is not tourist season, even in a tourist town. They are locals mostly – bundled-up mothers with less-than-school-aged children, senior citizens with nothing else to do. In this part of Victoria, the waterfront streets are lined with condominiums. During the warm tourist months, double-decker buses wind their way regularly from downtown to this Oak Bay attraction via the scenic, waterfront Dallas Road that follows the curves of the city's shore. In winter, the tourists are few and far between and the buses are a rare sight. Only now do the locals venture to see the sights. What else is there to do in February? They have bought annual passes at reduced rates, so that time and time again they can watch the three huge whales swim around the tiny pool, jumping up to the ring in the center, falling back amongst the others with a thrilling splash.

The trainer walks the whales through their routine, the same routine every day: slapping their tails, speaking, splashing with their fins, breaching, spyhopping, speed-swimming. These are the whales' natural activities, she says. This is what they do in the wild. This aquarium considers itself progressive. No longer are whales made to jump through hoops or leap over ropes. Progressive. The three huge whales in a pond built for one.

The show is over, so people are turning away when the trainer falls into the water.

At this aquarium, the trainers are forbidden to be in the water with the whales. Did she feel the tiny thrill of breaking the strictest rule?

The children look up, surprised, as the girl in blue splashes into the green-glass pool – her blonde hair floats around her head in a halo. She sinks before she swims, all those heavy clothes and boots pulling her down towards the concrete floor that is marked with algae and chipped paint. Children's faces look up, pressed against the glass, leaving nose prints, a trace of eyelashes.

The whales are there in an instant. In a heartbeat. One child starts to cry, but no one looks away. If they had been upstairs, in the crisp cold February air, they would have heard her scream as she surfaced. As her head broke through the water, surrounded by the bent dorsal fins and impossibly smooth black skin of three orcas – the whales called killer. Maybe she screams: "Get them away from me." Or something more obvious: "Help, someone help."

"I don't think this is supposed to happen," whispers a little girl with hair the color of an open flame.

They watch in silence.

Probably, the trainer had just been cleaning up, collecting the empty buckets once full of fish used to tempt the giant creatures up out of the water, used to lure them to slap their fins and swim on their backs like water-bound circus clowns. There must have been a splash when she hit the water, breaking the dark green stillness. She probably laughed when she first surfaced, surprised. How clumsy! To fall in. Especially in February, when it is so cold.

People stop. Someone takes a picture. "Is this part of the show?" someone else asks.

No.

Maybe when the black-and-white shadows first loom

underneath her, she pushes aside her fear and thinks: What an opportunity, to swim with the whales. Maybe she thinks, fleetingly, what a good story this will be later, when she is pulled out of the pool laughing and shivering.

Maybe she doesn't scream until she feels the tug on her leg, looks down and sees the cavernous mouth opening.

It happens awfully fast. It happens in slow motion. The children stand quietly, eyes upturned to the surface, their mouths falling open in silent O's.

They watch the one whale with the girl in his mouth.

To be held so gently in the mouth of the whale may first have felt like an embrace. But she is fighting, she is trying to reach for the life ring that is extended to her, the pole, anything. All around the pool, staff are banging buckets and blowing whistles. Can she hear their laughter turn to panic? Can she tell that the ring is out of reach?

When the whale lets go, she swims towards the edge. From underneath, the children watch her swimming – powerful strokes that churn the water. They are relieved. It's over. The frantic teacher herds them away, high-pitched voices ricocheting around the tunnel. In the pool, the girl's hands reach out to the aqua-blue stage she has so recently fallen off. She feels the cold, rough surface biting into her freezing flesh. She reaches up and up towards an outstretched hand, towards safety.

She screams when the tooth punctures her thigh.

What are the whales thinking? Some ancient instinct

to swim faster and deeper pulses through their captive hearts. Or is it a game? They have never seen anything in the water before but toys and food, and, of course, each other. Always, each other. Every time they turn around, when they are in the big pool, they see each other. Nothing else.

Maybe they are a little crazy.

Hearing the second scream, the blood-curdling scream that makes her own blood freeze, the teacher tries to rush the children up the ramp to the outside. There suddenly seems to be so many of them, slipping out of her control like a darting school of silver fish. Little faces stay clamped to the glass. The whales swim round and round, the girl trapped firmly in one giant jaw.

There is something about these whales most people don't know: At night, they are kept in a holding pen that is too small to swim in. There is some fear on the part of management that they will otherwise escape, or be freed, released into the open water from which they were stolen.

Sometimes, in the morning, cuts and scrapes fleck their shiny skins. Sometimes they exhale plumes of blood out their blowholes. The trainers quit, and write rancorous letters to the owners, but nothing changes. The whales bob up and down, held helplessly in place, unable to turn or move or feel the familiar cold current of the water on their skin.

Maybe they are a little angry.

Faster and deeper they go now in a pool that is often said to be no bigger than a bathtub. (It's so cruel, people say, after they pay their money to come in, to keep such magnificent creatures in a pool no bigger than a bathtub. But then they come back. Again and again.)

Three slippery-quick children have escaped the teacher's eye, stay hidden in the corner and watch as the girl stops struggling. It seems impossible for them to move or look away. They can see her face. How can they avert their gazes? They stare up through the swirling green water as though from the bottom of a dream.

Of course, she drowns. The pool is deep enough for that.

Maybe right up to the end she was thinking: What a story this will make.

Maybe she never looked up at the surface of the water from below and realized, as it spiraled around her, that she could not reach. That she would never be able to reach that surface again.

It takes ten hours to retrieve her naked body from the pool. The whales have stripped off all her clothes.

Later that night, the children from the school sit around their dinner tables, bent over meals of chicken and potatoes, and relay the story again and again, as though it was an exciting movie only they got to see. The parents of these children let them watch the story on the news. Other children sit alone in their rooms, silent and scared. Some don't tell their parents at all.

Three particular children wrap up the image of the girl's face as she stopped struggling, and bundle it deep inside where no one will ever be able to reach.

Tomorrow, counselors will be brought in to make them better. To try to make them forget. It will not be possible.

Months later, the Seaquarium gets shut down. The city refuses to renew the lease.

The whales are sold. The rest of the place, with the seal hospital and big fish tanks, is towed further north, to a new town.

In this city they will never again have whales in tanks no bigger than a bathtub.

ONE

In her dreams, there is always water.

It is never turquoise and blue and full of promise as it is in the South Pacific or the Mediterranean or even Grand Cayman, where her parents used to take her every year before they adopted Xav. Instead, the dream water is green-black and forbidding, thick as pea soup yet strangely clear, translucent, and sometimes glowing with a phosphorescent light.

The dream usually starts out to be safe: on land, inside buildings, at school, at the mall. Sometimes she can fly, tilting and angling above farmers' fields patched together like giant quilts. Sometimes she runs, and her feet skim along the grass without touching it and she can smell dew and moist soil and pine trees and sunshine. Sometimes she dances without effort, unable to feel the familiar tug of muscles gasping for oxygen, spinning across stage after endless stage. It doesn't matter how it starts, because always, without fail, no matter where she is, at some point in the night she finds herself near the bottle-green water, finds herself looking down and seeing the black-and-white shapes forming deep below her. Sometimes the giant dorsal fins break the green-glass surface and tower above her. Sometimes she hears the explosive puff of a blowhole. Sometimes a tail will appear to slap down on the calm water, forcing a dazzling white spray.

The strange part about her dreams is this: She always gets into the water. She falls, or jumps, or dives with the grace of an athlete, as though she is being pulled in by a force more powerful than a magnet and certainly more powerful than herself. There they are: black and white, black and white, so far below, looming closer. The black-and-white shapes become whales. She can see the white patch over their eyes, the grey patch behind the fin, the white belly, smooth and hard as armor. As they swim and dance in slow-motion arcs and twists, she is at first mesmerized by their beauty and grace, by the way they turn so silently in the water. Despite her pounding heart, she reaches out to touch their rubbery thick skin as they swim closer and closer. She feels the current they create pulling her legs, pulling.

Then she remembers – too late. She realizes her mistake; her heart starts to pound faster. She struggles to keep her head above the surface, knowing that from below the surface can look very far away. She tries not to look down, but her eyes seem to be able to focus nowhere else. The whales squeak and squeal under the water, a whistling that reverberates through her bones, echoes in her skull. Her head goes under, once, twice. At the surface, she looks frantically for a way to get out, but always, always, the shore has slipped away and she is left in the middle of a seaweed-green ocean, staring at her arm or leg or torso trapped in the grinning wide black-and-white mouth of an orca. She wakes up sweating. Her blankets are soaked with fear. It's the same every night.

Her name is Cassidy. Cassie.

Cassie has dreamt of whales every night for nine years. Since she was eight years old, every time she closes her eyes the tide of her sleep drags her out to sea and there she is again and again and again. She assumes she must be going crazy, that this is enough to make her crazy, yet she can't tell anyone, least of all her parents.

Her parents. Ha.

She only sees them on school holidays, even less now that she stays at the school year-round to attend the summer dance camps. And when she goes home, things usually escalate from small talk to a big fight and nothing gets talked about. Not that she'd tell them anyway. They've heard a lot worse stories than hers, she knows. She doesn't have any problems compared to some people.

You would think it would be easy for her to talk to them. After all, Cassie's parents are both in the listening business. Her mother is a psychiatrist, or was, before she had to take time off on her eternal "stress leave." Her father is the only one still working: Dr. Wagner, Alternative Therapy. He's not even a real psychiatrist. He's just a man with a sign in front of his house and an ad in the Yellow Pages. They are always saying things like, "*Cassie's so strong and determined, she hardly even needs parents; she was born an adult.*" The way her mother says it sounds bitter: "*Cassie's always known what she wanted; she never needed our guidance.*" But to Cassie herself, she says: "We all can't be dancers. You should probably have something to fall back on. Like I did."

Cassie thinks they might be mad that she doesn't seem to need them for anything, but she does! She's only seventeen. She wishes they were different, more like her roommate Sina's parents, who are always calling and sending care packages. Homemade cookies and hand-knit gloves and even, once, a photo album of family pictures.

Her parents never even call. They're all wrapped up in Xav and his problems. He was a foster child that they adopted, a drug baby, and now he is a little slow and has a wild temper and sometimes has seizures. She loves Xav, of course she does, it's just that he takes up *all* their time and effort. And he's really, really cute, which doesn't help – cute in a way that is usually reserved for baby animals. They fawn over him like he's a puppy, with his wild curly hair and huge black eyes and barely controlled personality. She feels like the giant ugly stepsister most of the time – big and gangly and hard-edged and old. She gets so angry and hurt that she wants to hit Xav or lock him in a closet. She certainly doesn't try anymore to treat her brother nicely. Most of the time she is just completely left out. It makes her feel detached, like she is in an invisible bubble that keeps her hovering just outside her family's life.

Cassie is expected to take care of herself. After all, she doesn't have any real problems.

"Help me," she imagines herself saying to them. "Please."

"How does that make you feel?" her father would ask her then. She's heard him asking the same thing of client after client in the front room. *How does that make you feel?* Cassie knows that sometimes he doesn't listen to their answers, his eyes taking him outside, thinking about the garden or dinner or what time Xavier will be home from school. He's laughed about it with them, later at dinner.

"She must have talked for half an hour and I didn't

hear a thing she said," he said once. "But it helps her just to talk about it; that's the best therapy in the world."

Are you serious? Cassie wants to ask him. *Really?* She feels sick, thinking about it now. She can imagine pouring her heart out to a stranger, thinking he was listening, thinking he could understand and help her, yet her own father ... There is no one to trust.

Her heart skips and jumps in her chest. Her fists lie clenched by her side.

Breathe, she reminds herself, pulling in a lungful of the cool, soft air.

Her fingers trace the tense muscles of her abdomen under the fine layer of sleep sweat. To calm herself, she counts her ribs, rippling just under the surface – the cage that keeps her heart from exploding, that keeps her secret inside. She has no one to tell.

Talking about it is the best therapy in the world. Maybe so, but she isn't talking.

Besides, she reminds herself, it's stupid. It happened a long time ago.

In the half-light of her room the dream fades away and seems less scary. She is in her dorm room in Vancouver, BC. Moonlit shadows slip over her desk and bureau and Sina's identical desk and bureau on the opposite wall. She is miles from the ocean that separates Vancouver from Victoria. In Vancouver, you can live in a city surrounded by water for years without ever going to the beach. In Victoria, it was different.

The city was smaller and the beaches encroached upon the town and everywhere you looked there was water. Dark green water filled with killer whales and other unknown shapes lurking deep below the surface. Vancouver is alive with buildings and stores and parks and traffic and restaurants and everything you can imagine. Cassie never goes to the beach in Vancouver. She doesn't have time, and besides, why bother? The only time she used to go was to walk her dog, Max, and he had to stay home with her parents. Dogs aren't allowed at boarding schools, no matter how progressive the school might be.

Cassie rarely even looks at the ocean except when she is traveling home on holidays on the big ferries. Even then, she doesn't look out the window when the ferry stops to observe orcas frolicking in the Strait. She goes directly to the newsstand and buys piles of glossy magazines and buries her head in them for the full hour and a half until the boat bumps the dock near Victoria.

She rolls over in bed and stares at the green glow of the alarm clock. Four-forty-five. She closes her eyes and inhales deeply, searching for just a bit more of that elusive sleep. This time, she promises herself, I won't get in the water. Across the room, Sina sighs noisily and turns over, dragging her quilt over her face. Without looking, Cassie can picture Sina's long black braid hanging down onto the floor, resting on a pile of clothes that are either just on the way to the laundry or just on the way back. Sina is a laundry junkie – she does laundry once a day, at least. The good thing about it is that she does Cassie's laundry, too. Their room always smells fresh and new, like detergent and something else, something warmer. It makes Cassie feel almost like she is still at home, her mother dutifully fluffing and folding for her. It makes her feel that someone is taking care of her.

Outside in the crisp fall air, she can hear cars beginning to arrive, tires squelching on the rain-soaked pavement. The kitchen staff are here. They always arrive early to prepare the daily meals for the boarders, and hot lunches for the day students. There is so much food here, it's ridiculous. The school takes pride in everything, from their balanced curriculum to its balanced nutritional regime. It really is a good school, Cassie agrees. She loves it here; it's where she belongs. She feels much more at home here than she ever felt at her real home.

She lies still and the wet sheets stick to her legs. She keeps her eyes closed and wills herself to go back to sleep, tossing and turning in the damp cotton.

Finally, she gives up and opens her eyes and watches the shadows of the pine and fir trees dance across the ceiling in the half-light. The rain has stopped and she can hear the stillness settle again outside. The school is located just outside of the city, buried in behind a suburb in a stand of fragrant old Douglas firs, cedars and exotic pine trees. Sometimes, the girls climb up the back hill and stand and look at the smog hanging over the metropolitan area and feel far removed from the bustling heart of Vancouver. At the same time, it's nice to be close to such an exciting place, a place where important ballet companies frequently perform.

"I'm getting up," she whispers.

She pushes the sheets back and tiptoes over to the closet that the girls share and pulls out her dance bag, all ready to go. It always is. There is no one else in the corridors as she makes her way quietly down to the studio. This is really the best time of day, she thinks, the constant din of girls' voices hushed by sleep. Through the doorways in the dorm, she can hear small snores and sighs. She envies their dreams, whatever they may be.

In the studio, the dawn light is beginning to filter in through the tall windows. Cassie changes quickly, not liking the musty smell of the change room, the way the walls seem to close in with no windows to break the darkness. It's hard to breathe in there; her chest feels tight, like she is underwater. Hurriedly, she knots her curly red hair into a loose bun at the nape of her neck. If it were a real dance class, she would have to take the time to scrape it down against her scalp, hold it prisoner with pins and gel and elastics, making a proper dancer's bun – Madame is very strict about appearances. But now there is no teacher, no other students.

The studio is silent – she doesn't want to wake anyone else. Sounds carry through the paper-thin wall that separates the theater and the studios from the boarding house. Since the first time she was lectured by the house mother, she has done her early-morning dancing in absolute quiet, accompanied only by her own ragged breathing and the sound of her slippers against the wood floor. She begins stretching and bending at the barre, her arms and legs slowly warming in the light. She concentrates all her effort into feeling each muscle, moving each limb with absolute precision. Watching herself in the mirror, she forces herself to repeat all the moves she finds most difficult as well as those that are so simple she can do them in her sleep. *Pliés, battements, ronds de jambe, adagios.* Her legs ache pleasurably. She breathes deeply in the dusty sunrise, feeling her lungs expand and contract. She is conscious of every pore of her body. She spends exactly one hour doing her barre exercises, one hour to the minute.

Then, instead of following the rigid routine of most rehearsals, she lets her body decide what to do. She loses herself in the silent dance, not watching herself as she twirls and leaps through the mirror's reflections and the early-morning sun, not noticing the worried face in the window from the hall that follows her every move.

It's almost seven o'clock in the morning. She's already been up for two hours. That means she had only a few hours' sleep last night, and she can feel her fatigue in her muscles and her joints. How can I keep going on such a small amount of sleep, she wonders. How long can this go on?

Rain spatters in giant drops on the windshield and the broken wipers swipe at it ineffectually as the tiny car ricochets wildly along the streets of Victoria. Dark green paint flakes off Holden's hands and onto the floor.

"That shit is gross, man. Can't you wash your hands?" Matt asks, with no small amount of hostility.

"Doesn't come off," he replies. "It's oil paint. Duh."

"Whatever. Don't get it all over my car."

"Right. Like it matters."

Holden surveys the floor of the yellow Volkswagen bug. McDonald's wrappers, cigarette packages, empty pop tins and crumpled paper completely obscure the floor mats. The thing smells like a garbage dump. He opens the window and hangs his head outside and lets the cold rain splash his skin.

"What are you doing, man? It's freezing in here," Matt snaps, reaching across and rolling the window up, the yellow car weaving and swerving through the traffic.

"Try not to kill us," Holden says, settling back in his seat.

He kicks the pile of junk on the floor. Junk. He reaches down and picks up a piece of lined paper that has one short sentence scrawled across the top.

"Hey, Matt," he says over the sound of the sputtering engine, "I think you forgot to do your history assignment."

Matt shows no sign that he has heard, cutting across two lanes of traffic to get into the McDonald's drive-through. Holden sighs and drops his head back. Absently he picks at the paint flakes on his hands, ignoring Matt's scathing glance. His head is aching and his stomach is churning as the tiny car skids, barely avoiding a cyclist in the driveway.

"It's a *drive*-through, not a bike-through," yells Matt out the window, laughing maniacally. "*Idiot! Ban the bike! Ban the bike!* Hey, Holden, let's start a *ban the bike* movement! It'll be cool, like the sixties. We'll have a protest march. It's the nineties version: Ban the bike!"

Holden sighs.

"What's your problem, man?"

"Nothing," says Holden. "Headache."

"Huh," says Matt, without much sympathy. "You shouldn't drink so much."

"I know. Shut up."

"Well, you shouldn't," Matt says.

"Yeah? Well, you shouldn't eat so much."

"Oh, nice. Thanks, man."

"Lay off," Holden moans. "Please."

The two friends sit, not speaking, staring moodily at the bumper of the car in front of them. A bumper sticker reads: If you can read this, you're too close. Matt laughs.

"That's funny. If you can read this, you're too close. Don't you think? Funny. It's not my favorite, though. Best one is: Mean people suck. I want one of those."

Holden doesn't bother responding. He glances over at his friend. Matt looks exactly the same as he did when they were kids: round, freckled face and blonde, curly hair that springs out from his scalp at strange angles. The freckles camouflage the zits, he thinks nastily. The most noticeable difference is that now Matt is, well, a lot bigger. He is so tall he has to half-crouch in the little car, his knees practically bent up to his ears. And he's not fat, exactly, but certainly not the gangly kid he once was. Okay, maybe he is fat. His chin wobbles slightly as he talks.

"Shut up," says Holden quietly.

"What?"

"Nothing."

The car vibrates in the long lineup. The rain stops abruptly and gusts of wind whip the sky open. Daylight sneaks through into the blue clearing. Holden closes his eyes against the bright September sun that reflects off every wet, shiny surface at just the right angle to penetrate his hung-over brain. He read somewhere that you get a headache after you drink because your brain is actually shrunken from dehydration. His brain is probably beyond repair, he thinks miserably. Shrunk to the size of a frozen pea.

"Get me a large Coke, too," he says.

"You got any money?"

"Shit," says Holden unhappily. He doesn't have any money. Of course he doesn't. He pushes his straight brown hair out of his eyes. "Forget it."

"Just kidding, I'll get it. Don't worry about it."

"Thanks, money-bags."

Holden never has any money, while Matt is always flush. Both of Matt's parents work: His mom's a realtor and his dad is, of all things, a nurse. They give him a pretty good allowance and don't bug him too much about getting a job. Not like Holden's dad, who thinks he is a lazy slob. By the time *he* was sixteen, he'd had a hundred jobs, of course. Sure.

Basically, Matt has the perfect family. There are no skeletons in the closet, their lawn is always manicured, and there are always flowers in the pots on the front steps. Matt's mother is cheerful, and his dad is friendly and appears interested in what they are doing. He's always in the stands cheering for Matt in whatever tournament he happens to be playing in: basketball, soccer, football. Holden can even overlook the fact that he's a nurse, which isn't the greatest career choice in his opinion, because he's so cool. Yeah, he'd overlook *that* and trade fathers with Matt in a hot second.

Holden's dad gives him money only when he asks – which he hates to do – and it always comes with conditions. He has to make a list of what he's bought, to the penny, and keep a tally of what's left over. He has to show his dad that he's been trying to find work. It's almost like living with some kind of unemployment police. He's only sixteen! His dad's a lawyer, so he has plenty of cash; he just doesn't want to part with it. Also, he's just not that ... well, accessible. He goes away for weeks at a time and never tells Holden exactly why. Something to do with the work he does, some big-deal corporate law.

Holden's mom ... well, that's another story. His beautiful mom. She was amazing – a free spirit. She was the one who taught Holden how to paint when he was just a little kid. She let him use the good oil paints right away and never said that anything he did was stupid looking or a waste of time. How *she* hooked up with his dad, he'll never know. His dad was lucky to have her. She was gorgeous; she often looked like she was on her way out to a fancy dinner party or something. She could have been a Hollywood star. But they never went anywhere. She dressed up and stayed home while his dad worked, and she painted and made sculptures in the backyard and redecorated the house a million times.

One day he came home from school and found that she had left. Gone. *Escaped*, was the word she used in her note, scrawled across the tabletop in indelible ink. It was still there, under the cloth. His dad said she had a problem with drugs. Frankly, Holden can't imagine it – his mom, a junkie. He hasn't seen her for almost five years, during which time the house has taken on a look of decay that is unmatched in the neighborhood. It's Holden's job to clean it, but he rarely bothers. And his dad doesn't even care. Why should Holden worry if his dad doesn't? He's only sixteen.

He presses his eyes closed harder, making his head hurt even more, and thinks about the painting he was working on last night. There is something not quite right in the swirling green of the ocean, something he can't pinpoint. Maybe Matt's right. Obviously Matt's right. He *shouldn't* drink so much. Maybe the painting would come easier without the Wild Turkey. His stomach leaps and twists, remembering. He must have passed out, because he didn't clean up his brushes and palette like he usually does, and when he woke up this morning on the couch in the attic, he was still fully dressed and it felt like he had a mouth full of wool. And a head full of nails. The brushes are probably ruined, and he hardly has the money to buy new ones. Unless he asks his dad again.

I'm going to quit drinking, he promises himself. I'm quitting right now.

"Shit," he whispers.

"What is your *problem*?"

"Nothing."

Holden reaches over and turns up the radio. The Bee Gees fill the silence.

"Hey," says Matt, cranking the volume. "Who would

have thought AM radio would be cool again?"

They roll up to the order mike, clouds of blue smoke puffing from the exhaust pipe of the noisy car.

"Two happy meals, two coffees, four orders of hash browns and a large Coke!" Matt shouts, his good mood returning with the thought of breakfast.

Holden keeps his eyes firmly shut, watching the pattern of sunlight through the back of his eyelids. Dark red, like blood. His stomach is burning now and he feels pretty sick. Coffee is probably not a great choice. He's all of sixteen and he's getting an ulcer. Behind his closed eyes, his painting haunts him. There is either too much light, or not enough. Or maybe it's the shadows – too big, or too small. How would he know? He's never been in the ocean, except when he was little, and then he was floating on the top, not swimming underneath. If he's going to make a living painting underwater scenes, he should probably get his feet wet. Shit.

"You ever go scuba diving?"

"Nope." Matt laughs. "Have *you*?"

"I might try it."

"Yeah, right. You. Ha ha, that's funny. You're afraid of water, remember? Wimp? Besides, you don't even know how to *swim*."

"I used to. When I was a kid. I used to know how to swim. I don't think that's something you *forget*."

"Well, I haven't forgotten, but *you* ... "

"What the hell is that supposed to mean? I can swim."

"Whatever. I've always wanted to scuba dive myself. I just thought you were too ... "

"Too *what*, asshole?"

"I don't know, I thought you were freaked out."

They stare at each other.

"They teach you in the public pool. I mean, it's not as if you're out in the ocean – not right away."

Matt bites into his hash brown, grease glistening on the corners of his lips.

"If you want to go for it," he says, "I'm there with you, man. Just don't freak out and drown or some stupid shit like that. Don't embarrass me."

"Me? Embarrass *you*? Jerk."

"I'm signing us up, Holden. Don't change your mind. This'll be cool. I'm going to sign us up. I know a guy. This'll be great."

Holden sips his coffee and grimaces as it belts into his gut, hot and painful. Scuba diving. Well, he can't back out now. He'll quit drinking and overcome his fears all at the same time. He'll be a new person. Suddenly he is ravenous. He bites enthusiastically into the salty egg.

"We're going to be late," he says, not really caring. "We're going to be late, again."

Back on the busy streets of Vancouver, Mark Mitchell makes his way against the flow of traffic from downtown out towards St. Catherine's Girls' School for the Arts. He can't get used to the idea of being a teacher, even though it is his second year at St. Cat's, as it is affectionately known. It seems like just yesterday that he was a student himself, and he can sure relate more to the students than the teachers. Most of his colleagues at the school are artists and actors and dancers turned teachers at "retirement" from their artistic careers, so they are much older than him and seem to occupy a whole different world. In fact, he is still puzzled about why he was hired at all. He got his teaching degree years ago, when he was twenty-four, but he never used it until last year. He had devoted his life to being an anti-captivity activist, and spent most of his time leading protest groups and publishing literature to educate the public.

Now, trapped in his station wagon in the river of traffic, he's not even sure why he applied for *this* job, or why he took it, or even if he enjoys it at all. He likes the school; he likes the way the students are encouraged to think "outside the box" and to get involved with whatever they are passionate about. The hours work for him as well; he leads his protests during summer vacation and winter break and has passed much of the legwork on to volunteers. And, he thinks wryly, the teaching salary pays the rent, and now that his wife is expecting ... well, he has to think of that.

His problem is mostly that he gets too attached to the students. The classes are so small, it's impossible not to get to know them: The school goes from grades one through twelve and has only five hundred students. There is one student in particular to whom he feels an odd sort of parental responsibility towards. Her name is Cassie Wagner. He is particularly interested in her for one purpose: She was one of the witnesses to the worst accident at an aquarium in Canadian history. The same accident, in fact, that turned the tables for him and led him to be an advocate of freeing whales from captivity.

Mark Mitchell's younger brother, Todd, had been the first to work at the Seaquarium. He had seen it coming, the accident. He had seen the way the whales were treated, and the way the whales were reacting, and was always coming home from work stressed and worried. Mark had started working there himself, as a janitor of all things, just to see what Todd had been so upset about. It wasn't difficult: A couple of times trainers fell in the water and had to be pulled away from the whales quickly; the huge beasts had been reluctant to let them go. Also, if the whales did not perform adequately, in the opinion of management, their food was withheld and they were kept overnight in pens so small they couldn't turn around. Mark was shocked. Todd had finally written letters to management, and when they were ultimately ignored, he had quit his job. And right before his two weeks' notice was up, it had happened. He had confronted the manager – he had said, "See?"

"It was a horrible accident," the manager had said,

and then repeated that statement to the press. "A horrible, unexpected accident."

Mark is interested in Cassie Wagner because she has never talked about what happened, as much as he tries to bring it up in class. He watches her turn away at the mere mention of marine biology. He sees her fall asleep in class. He wants to talk to her about it because it seems like she would be the perfect spokesperson for ...

Well.

He can't think of that now. It is a sunny morning in September and he is running late for school. He rolls down the window and the cool air pours into the car. He breathes deeply and tries to ignore the smell of all that exhaust, polluting everything it touches. He edges along in the traffic, making a note to himself to start arriving earlier, to beat the rush hour.

TWO

"Hey, Cassie! Cassie!"

Sina is out of breath, as usual, always in a hurry to do something or go somewhere.

Cassie slows her pace to allow her friend to catch up. They are making their way back to the boarding house after a late basketball practice. It's not raining, for a change, and the setting sun is filtering through the elegant pine needles and heavy oak branches and casting rippling shadows on the path. It looks almost pretty. Cassie's feet crunch along the gravel in her clunky basketball shoes. Big piles of sodden, fallen leaves are clumped beside the trail. Cassie is in a bad mood. She hates basketball – the way you have to slam your body around the court, pounding down on your knees and ankles in a totally graceless way – but it's better than sitting around in her room, waiting for school to start the next day.

Sina runs to catch up, her jacket flapping in the breeze.

"What's going on?" Cassie asks.

"Oh, right! I was talking to my mom last night? And she says that if you want you can come to our place for Thanksgiving?"

Cassie smiles. "That'd be great, Sina, really, but I think my mom would just about kill me if I didn't go home. If I wasn't there, who would she pick on?"

"Really?" Sina says, her disappointment showing on her face. She sweeps the shiny curtain of hair back behind her ear. "Really? Because I was thinking we could, you know, hang out."

"Sina, we hang out all the time."

"I know, I just ... "

"Is something wrong?"

Sina shrugs. "I don't know. It's just ... it'll be so weird at home without my dad. It'll be just me and my mom, you know? My sisters are staying in England; they said they'd be home for Christmas. So Thanksgiving. I don't know. It'll just be weird, you know?"

Sina's father works overseas at an oil refinery in Saudi Arabia. He's always been home for holidays, and because Sina goes to boarding school, the fact that he is away most of the time doesn't really affect her that much.

"Oh Sina, that's a drag. I'm sorry. You could come to

my place ... not that you'd want to. But you're welcome," Cassie says, reaching out to touch her friend's arm.

"And leave my mom alone? I couldn't. Thanks. I couldn't."

The girls walk quietly, listening to the sound of cars pulling out of the lot, kicking the loose leaves under their feet. Cassie's ballet-damaged feet are sore in the loose sports shoes. It seems they are always either swollen or bleeding, and they are so ugly with huge calluses and corns from dancing *en pointe*. She wiggles her toes as she walks to release the cramps.

"You know what, Cass? I need a cigarette. You want to come?"

Behind the primary school playground, there is a small cluster of trees that the girls refer to as the Woods. It is really no more than a dozen or so Douglas firs, but the trees are huge. Old growth, they have been told. They provide a great canopy for the girls to gather under, madly smoking contraband cigarettes at every opportunity, hidden from the matron's eyes.

Cassie hates to smoke, but she likes the group – the laughter and talking, the feeling that they're apart from the school. Still, every time she does it, she gets panicky afterwards. What is she doing to her body? Will her lungs turn black and fill with cancer? Will it affect her dancing? Sometimes it makes her lightheaded and dizzy, which in turn makes her feel both anxious and stupid. She feels like she's pretending to be grown up, when inside she's just a little kid who should be climbing on the monkey bars or swinging on the rope or something. She looks over at Sina, who looks, if at all possible, even more beautiful through a veil of blue smoke. Elegant and sophisticated. She claims she was born in the wrong era, in the wrong place, that she was meant to be a Parisian in the twenties, smoking lavender cigarettes through alabaster holders.

Of course, Sina is an actress. Tomorrow she may be a hippie flower child. A punk rocker from the eighties.

"Sure," Cassie says, hiding her distaste. She links her arm through Sina's. "Let's go smoke our lungs out!"

The girls disappear into the Woods, laughing. Neither of them feels Mr. Mitchell's eyes watching from the parking lot across the drive; neither of them sees him shaking his head. He gets into his car and drives away slowly, thoughtfully.

It's a different life for him, here, at this performing arts school. Because he teaches biology and not something more relevant like singing or dance, he often is ignored completely. He is working on a project right now that he hopes will involve the students and maybe spark their interest: a sort of combination of creativity and science. He sighs. He has to think of a way to encourage them to be involved.

The traffic is heavy and it will take him hours to get home. He detours right and then left and steers the little car down to the water, where he sits for a long time looking out at the harbour. Somewhere out there, he thinks, they're free.

Far away from Vancouver and out of sight, a pod of whales makes its way north off the coast of Vancouver Island. Twenty-four strong, the animals move steadily, their breathing synchronized, their bodies rising and falling as smoothly as gears in a clock. Earlier, they passed a bright orange boat filled with whale watchers, and their images have been caught on dozens of cameras. They performed only by passing by, breaching, perhaps, or spyhopping. Nothing more. Freely, they moved on, unbarricaded in the endless expanse of the Pacific Ocean. Unstoppable.

Holden sits in the change room at the Victoria Y, holding his crisp new swimsuit in his hands, his jeans and paint-stained T-shirt sticking to his skin like glue. He is sitting because the multicolored tiles are tipping and sliding beneath his feet. "Shit," he says out loud, as he drops his head towards his knees. He didn't even drink last night, and he has a hangover anyway. Maybe he always has one, he just doesn't notice. His shrunken brain and all that. The room spins.

As usual, they were late, mostly because Matt was late to pick him up. One day he has to get his own ride

– Matt is, at best, really unreliable. Of course, Matt is already in the water and Holden is still in the change room. Holden shakes his head firmly and forces himself to step out of his street clothes into the new trunks, inhaling deeply the once-familiar heavy scent of chlorine. The trunks feel cold and strange against his skin.

It's just a pool, he reminds himself. No big deal. Just a pool. Matt has already dashed off to join the class, sporting a pair of designer trunks on his oversized body. Holden can hear him laughing, even from here, his huge belly laugh echoing around the pool. He's probably telling them that Holden's too afraid to join them, that he's a real wimp with a fear of phantom whales.

He reaches into his bag and pulls out the mickey of assorted liquor he has siphoned off his dad's supply. Swamp water. It burns as it goes down his throat, leaping into his gut with a hot kick. Two more swallows, and he feels a little better. Better enough to stand up and walk coolly over to the shower to get wet before making his entrance. Better enough that he can talk louder than the voice in his head that is reminding him that he doesn't have to do this. Why is he doing this?

"It's just a pool," he says out loud, stepping out onto the pool deck.

"Yeah," says a voice behind him. "It's not the pool that's scary, it's what comes next: the ocean."

"Thanks for reminding me," he says, half jumping out of his skin. He turns around.

The girl behind him is tall and thin and is clutching a towel to her chest. Her blue eyes spark and glitter in the bright lights.

"I can't do this," she says.

"How come?"

"Sharks," she says seriously.

"What?"

"Sharks. It's stupid. You're going to laugh, so go ahead. It's just that ... "

"What?"

"I don't know. I have this really irrational fear of sharks. My mom signed me up for this so that I could get over it, but you know, I don't think this is the way."

"Yeah," says Holden.

"So, what's yours?"

"My what?"

"Why do you have to talk yourself into this?"

"Whales," he says, and laughs sheepishly. "Irrational fear of whales."

"Let's bail," she says. "This isn't worth it."

"Exactly," says Holden. "Let's get out of here."

I don't need to do this, he rationalizes, as he rushes back to his locker and throws his clothes back on. Art is art. I don't have to actually go underwater to paint what I see in my head. What difference does it make? Right away he feels calmer. He takes a reassuring swig from the almost-empty flask and his knees stop shaking. He tries to avoid looking at himself in the mirror.

He can't. He sees himself, a dark-haired, skinny teenager with a sharp jaw and small nose. He pulls his hair down over his dark eyes. Better. The pool might not have been a big deal, but that girl was right: the ocean was a big deal. Well, that's over, he thinks. I don't have to do that.

He makes his way up into the stands with a bag of Fritos. The smell of the chorine is almost comforting from this distance. He remembers his shiny blue swim trunks with the neat little row of badges his mom sewed on after each session. Of course, that was before she ... well. He eats another mouthful of the salty chips. The first time he went to swimming lessons, the teacher held his face underwater to prove to him he could do it and he came up gasping and screaming. Chlorine burned his eyes.

Maybe it wasn't such a great memory after all.

He scans the pool and finds the familiar bulk of Matt. Matt waves and dives back into the water in a show-offy way, giving Holden the thumbs-up signal. Holden waves back, half-heartedly clapping.

"That's my boy," he calls. "Yahoooooo!"

"I feel bad," the girl says, plonking herself down next to him.

"Huh? Why?"

He glances over at her and barely recognizes her in jeans and a motorcycle jacket. She has pulled her hair back and her eyes are wide in her tanned face.

"I was only trying to talk *myself* out of this," she

says. “I wasn’t trying to drag anyone else back with me.”

“No big deal,” Holden shrugs. “Really, I didn’t want to go anyway.”

“If it weren’t for me, would you have?” she asks.

“Nah,” says Holden, offering her a chip. “I thought I needed to, but it turns out I didn’t.”

They sit and watch in companionable silence while the class in the pool learns about the basics of breathing through the regulators and little tricks like spitting on their masks to stop them from fogging up. Holden tries to concentrate and finds that he can’t. He’s pleasantly buzzed from the liquor, and the chips are delicious and salty on his tongue. He congratulates himself on dropping out. The class sounds way too complicated. He did the classroom work with Matt last week, and, in theory, it sounded easy. But now he can hardly remember it. He’s glad he’s not embarrassing himself in the pool. Buoyancy and mask cleaning. Breathe through your mouth. Don’t do this, try to do that. Whatever. The class bobs around the pool like ridiculous diseased fish.

The same guy that taught the classroom part of the course outlines the dive schedule – pool dives, shallow-water dives, then, finally, a deep-ocean dive from a boat.

“Wow,” the girl says. “I’m glad it’s not me. I know I would have panicked in the ocean and probably forgotten everything and drowned or got the bends or something.”

"Who are you here with?" Holden asks, to make conversation.

"Oh. Me? I'm here with my mom. She's over there in the red."

"Cool," says Holden. "Your mom."

"She is cool," says the girl defensively. "Really," she adds.

"I wasn't saying she wasn't."

"No, I mean, she really is. She's a triathlete. I was going to train with her, but I don't know about the swimming. Well, obviously. I can swim. I just don't like it that much. I mean ... I swim in the pool all the time. But in the meet I was going to train for, the swimming part is in the ocean. I just ... well. I'll probably be able to swim really fast, if nothing else. My mom thought it would be better if I wasn't really ... panicky."

"Yeah," says Holden. "I know what you mean."

"Who's your friend?" she asks, after a pause.

"My friend?"

"Yeah, that guy that's waving at you."

"Oh, that's Matt. He's great. He's, like, an athlete. You'd probably like him."

"You should introduce me, maybe."

"I don't even know your name."

"Oh," she laughs. "I'm Taylor."

After class, Holden finds Matt in the change room, making poses in the mirror.

"Looking good, my man," he is saying to himself in

the mirror. He admires the muscles cut into the side of his abdomen that are only visible when he holds his breath and sucks in his gut. "Lookin' good."

"Jerk," says Holden.

"Speak for yourself, my wimpy friend," Matt says. "I knew you wouldn't do it."

"Whatever, Tubby, get dressed. I've got someone I want you to meet."

He drags his friend out into the stands and looks around for Taylor. She isn't there. The stands are empty.

"Hey," he says, disappointed.

"Who was she?"

"No one. Just a girl. She was pretty cool."

"Why didn't *you* ask her out, then?"

"Not my type," Holden shrugs.

"Not like ... "

"Shut up, don't say it," Holden warns.

"Not like *Cassie*."

"God, Matt, how old are you, anyway? That was, like, five years ago. She doesn't even write to me anymore."

"Yeah? So how come you still keep the flame burning?"

"Shut up."

"Find me a great girl and then lose her before I get to meet her," Matt grumbles under his breath. "Some kind of friend you are."

THREE

"I can't go for dinner," Cassie says emphatically. "I have a dance practice tonight."

"Come on," Sina begs. "I hate eating alone. And it's lasagna night. You love lasagna ... think of all that gooey cheese and yummy sauce ... Come on ... "

"Sina, no. I can't, okay?"

Cassie is irritated and slightly sick from the cigarettes that she's been smoking again out behind the school. The smell has seeped into her hair, and every time she moves, she gets another waft of it. Everyone must be able to smell it, she thinks. She flunked a science test, and somehow she thought smoking would make her feel better. Ha. Each time she goes back behind the school with Sina, she regrets it. She always tries not to inhale, then feels like a total baby. Now she just feels like crying. At practice tonight, Madame Chantelle is going to choose the leads for the Christmas recital, and Cassie feels horrible and not like dancing at all.

"Can't you skip it for once?" Sina wheedles. "It's our last dinner before Thanksgiving."

"Sina, forget it. This is important."

They make their way down the long white hallway towards the cafeteria, their footsteps ringing hollowly, their voices resonating off the tile ceiling. There are only fifty boarders at the school. All the other girls are day students who get to go home for dinner every night, get to leave the building. Cassie looks out the window into the sun that is sinking into the heavy layer of clouds, coloring them all vivid orange and pink. Sometimes she feels like she is trapped here, like it's a prison. Not that she wants to go home to her loony family for dinner; not that it wouldn't be a three-hour trip even if she wanted to. She does miss her dog, though. That's the only thing. Sometimes she thinks it might even be worth it, the traveling, just to see Max. Her parents bought her Max when they brought Xav home for the first time. Well, they bought Max for Xav, too, but he was just a baby, so Cassie got to train him and he slept in her room, taking up most of the bed. She misses Max a lot, with his big brown eyes and floppy paws and loving gazes.

"Hey Sina," she starts, "do you ever think abo – "

Suddenly Sina freezes.

"Ssssh ... " she whispers, her tone changing completely. "Look who's coming!"

Cassie looks up. Familiar dark curly hair and dangerous black eyes. She groans. Mark Mitchell stops, smiling broadly.

"Good evening, girls. What are you doing here so late?"

"Just going for dinner, Mr. Mitchell," Sina chirps, flicking her long hair and fluttering her lashes. "What are you doing here?"

"Late staff meeting. You know how they are." He rolls his dark eyes dramatically, winking at Cassie. "What a drag. But at least I'll avoid the rush-hour traffic."

"Sure," she says, not knowing what else to say. "Great."

It's a well-known fact that about ninety-nine percent of the girls at St. Cat's are in love with Mark Mitchell. Cassie is in the one percent who couldn't care less. So he's cute – so what? He's old, at least thirty, and his hair is too long, curling over his collar like a hippie. And he teaches *biology*, which is a lot less than interesting in a school for the arts. Sina is positively simpering, which makes Cassie even more irritated than she was before.

"Look," she says, "I have to get to practice."

"Oh," says Mark. "Do you have dancing tonight?"

"Um, yeah. *Dancing*." She gives him as dirty a look

as she can muster. "See you, Sina," she tosses over her shoulder as she hurries down the corridor, her heart pounding.

If he is so nice, and so cute, why does he make me so uncomfortable? she wonders. She shudders. It's like he's looking right into my soul, like he knows all my secrets. She puts the thought away as she bursts into the dance studio and runs into the change room. The ten other girls are already stretching for barre exercises, and she doesn't want to be late on audition day. Especially not today. She knows she has a good chance at the role she wants, and she's heard that there will be some important people in the audience at the show. People she needs to impress. After all, she is seventeen. She's almost old, for a ballerina, and she needs to get into a good company by the end of the school year. She'll die if she doesn't, she thinks, tying the ribbon on her shoes. She *has* to get the part. She just has to. She flexes her leg and stretches down over it, touching her nose to her knees. Her muscles stretch and sigh. Better, she thinks. I feel better. She takes a deep breath and joins the others at the barre.

FOUR

"This is your brain on drugs," says Holden, splatting a big blob of green paint on the canvas. He takes one last pull on the roach.

"Yeah? At least I have a brain," says Matt, giggling. "A brain big enough to make a stain. Hey, I'm a poet and I don't even know it!"

He dissolves into full-blown laughter, tears threatening the corners of his eyes. "Poet! Know it! Get it?"

"Yeah," says Holden, squinting at his friend through the haze of smoke. "I get it. I just don't think it's funny."

For some reason this makes Matt laugh harder.

"You're killing me, man! Stop it! Get out of here!"

"Whatever."

"No, I mean it! Get out of here!" Matt howls.

"Matt, grow up," Holden groans.

"Screw you." Matt stops laughing abruptly. "Hey, let's go for a walk."

Holden looks out the window suspiciously, the weather confirming his nasty mood.

"It's *cloudy*," he says nastily.

"So?"

"I don't know. It looks cold."

"It's not cold. It's October, for god's sake. It's like, I don't know, balmy outside."

"Balmy?" repeats Holden. "Balmy? You're such a geek." He squints at his friend appraisingly. "Geek," he repeats. "All right, fine, we'll go outside in this balmy weather."

The two friends stumble down the stairs, the fresh fall air slapping them partway into sobriety. They walk in silence for a while, shoving and jostling, passing by rows of old houses and a tumbledown graveyard. On the other side of the graveyard is Dallas Road, winding its way along the waterfront of Victoria. The city has spent a lot of time and money building up the beach on the water side of Dallas Road, which is always getting washed away by winter storms. Once you cross the road, you can walk for miles along the beach with the traffic humming along at intervals right above you. They hang out there a lot in the summer and have fires and beach parties that are regularly shut down by the police. They've been going there since they were little kids, only the beach didn't used to go all the way along. They used to have to walk along the wall for part of the way. Everything changes, Holden thinks grumpily to himself. Everything gets messed with.

"So, tell me about Taylor," he says, trying to sound casual.

"What's to tell? You met her first, you know what she looks like."

"How'd *you* end up meeting her?"

"Oh, I got to talkin' to her mom. She's pretty cool. And she introduced us. What's it to you?"

"Well, you have like, well, never gone out with a girl before. I was just, you know, curious. What's her story?"

Matt shrugs, blushing. "I don't know. We're not going out or anything. I mean, we went out for food after practice the other night, no big deal. Her mom was there, for god's sake."

"Did ya lay some lip on her?"

He nudges Matt's arm, heavily, almost staggering, making kissy faces. Matt's face gets redder, like it's going to explode.

"Hey, lay off. Her mom was there. I told you that. What do you think?"

"Matt and Taylor sittin' in a tree," Holden chants. He can see Matt is getting upset, but for some reason he can't seem to stop himself. "K-I-S-S-I-N-G ... "

"You're just jealous," hisses Matt. "Lay *off*. I mean it, asshole."

"All right. Okay. You don't have to get hostile."

Matt shoves his friend onto a lawn, and Holden falls into a rose bush that has been cut back to a stump.

"Ouch!" Holden yells. He lies there for a couple of minutes. The rose stump bites into his back and he stares at the endless grey of the cloudy sky. "It is cold," he says grouchily. "I told you it would be."

"So I got chosen to be the lead in the 'Tourmente de Neige,' which is a new dance that Madame just choreographed, and it's great because it's really hard, but I know the steps, and I'll be onstage for at least twenty minutes, most of the time by myself, and ... "

Cassie lets her voice trail off and looks around the table at her family. Her mother is silently helping herself to another bowl of salad. She is always quiet when she is on a diet, and from the looks of her, she has been on this one for quite a while. Her collarbone is poking through her beige sweater. Of course, she gives no indication that she has heard anything her daughter has said. Her father is looking at her, which is a good sign, but instead of saying something about her dance, he starts talking about a new client he has who is only a teenager but has already tried to commit suicide four times and has been in rehab twice. Her brother – although she didn't expect a response from him, as he is only ten – focuses stonily on the TV behind her that is showing the parade with the sound off.

"Whatever," she says in response to her dad.

Angrily, she stuffs another mouthful of dry turkey into her mouth.

"I won a Nobel prize in chemistry," she says in the next silence. "Right after I cured cancer, I stumbled on the cure for Aids. Of course everyone was surprised. I mean, I know I'm only in high school ... "

Still no response. Her father moves his chair back from the table and stares at the mute TV. Her mother looks up for a minute and starts to say something, then goes back to chewing her lettuce like a starved rabbit.

"What were you going to say, Mother?"

"Oh, nothing, dear. Actually, I was just going to mention that if you want to be a dancer, you might want to have smaller helpings of turkey. You won't be able to maintain that physique forever, you know."

Cassie leans back. This is what it's like being the child of shrinks, she says to herself. How does that make you feel? She snorts derisively.

"I'm going out," she says, pushing her plate away.

"Bye," all three say in chorus.

They aren't even surprised. No one even asks her where she is going.

The fresh, cool air is a relief. Being in her house is suffocating – she can hardly breathe in there. Slowly, she wanders down the deserted road towards the new Dallas Road beach, dragging Max behind her. The wind blows her hair around her face, into her mouth and eyes. She ties it back in a ponytail with a piece of string in her pocket and shoves the rest under her knit hat.

"Come on, Max," she says impatiently, tugging the leash.

The big Great Dane just stares mournfully at her and continues galumphing along at the exact same rate as a snail, panting balefully.

"Hurry *up*!"

It's quite pleasant, for October, and the air smells familiar – like childhood and exhaust and lawn clippings and the greenish scent of trees. In the background, she can smell the cool saltiness of the beach. The leash bites into her hand as Max wanders around the sidewalk. Giving up, she slows her pace to match Max's, kicking leaves and pebbles as she goes.

"The whole family is nuts," she tells Max. "How does that make you feel? Hey, did I tell you I got the lead in the Christmas show? Wanna come watch? Huh? You'll have to take the ferry, but I'm sure you'll be fine. You can have Mom and Dad's seats – it's not like they'll use them."

The dog stops, and lifts his leg lazily on the neighbor's rose bush.

"Nice," says Cassie. "But at least you listened."

Holden and Matt climb over a pile of logs at the bottom of the stairs to the desolate beach. It's windy, and definitely colder near the water. And it stinks – some combination of rotting seaweed and wet wood. Holden shivers, wishing he had at least brought a jacket. Or a mickey. That's the good thing about drinking, he muses. It keeps you warm. There is no one else in sight except a grey-haired woman and a dog in the distance. He is about to suggest that they leave when he notices Matt staring out to sea.

"This is so beautiful," he says softly. "This is really great."

Holden tries not to seem surprised. It's not like Matt has ever been a great lover of scenery before. He shrugs. Girls. Whatever.

"Hey," he says, "let's run or something. To warm up." He reaches over and touches Matt on the arm, looking seriously into his eyes. "You're it!!!!" he screeches, laughing, and takes off down the beach, Matt close behind.

As they get closer to the woman, Holden realizes that it's not her hair that's grey, it's just a hat, a wool hat pulled low over her ears. In fact, her hair is long and red and curly, escaping from a loose ponytail. The dog looks at him forlornly before the girl turns around.

All three stop and stare at each other.

"Cassie?" says Matt, in disbelief.

"Holden?" she says, staring right into his eyes. "Matt?"

Matt breaks the silence first. "Wow," he says. "Cassie. What's new?"

They look at each other, and finally a smile cracks her pale face.

"Not much," she says. "You?"

"It's been a while, I guess," says Holden, smiling crookedly. "I guess it's been a while since we saw you." Impulsively, he reaches over and hugs her hard, feeling her bones through her thick wool sweater. "And might I add," he says, "you're looking really good."

"So, how come Matt couldn't come?" asks Cassie from across the booth.

"I don't know," Holden shrugs. "New girlfriend. I guess he doesn't have time for me anymore."

"Aw," she says. "Sad."

"Hey!"

"Just kidding. Lighten up, my friend."

Holden laughs, something he hasn't really done for a long time without being drunk. Or stoned. "I know. Sorry. I guess it's just weird not having him always hanging over my shoulder. Anyway, at least this way I get you all to myself."

She laughs. "Sure, whatever."

Whatever? Holden thinks, realizing he meant it. This is like a date. He looks over at her white freckled hand lying on the table and fights the urge to pick it up.

Obviously, she thinks of him as just a friend. He stares at her fingernails, ragged and chewed, until she notices and curls her hand into a fist.

"So, uh, when do you go back?"

"Oh, tomorrow. I have a major rehearsal. Actually, I just got this great part in the show we put on at Christmas and I can't wait to start practicing."

Holden watches her face as she describes the dance. In the bright lights of the restaurant her skin is paler than white behind her mask of freckles. Her vivid hair is loose and curls fly around her face. As she talks, her fingers trace out the dance on the table.

"I'm sorry," she says.

"What? Why?"

"Oh, you can't be interested in this. It's just... forget it. Let's talk about something else. Let's talk about you. What have you been up to since seventh grade?"

He grins. "Oh, not much. Just hangin' with Matt. You know."

"Oh."

"I've been doing some painting. A bit, you know, not as much."

"Really? You used to be so good, I remember."

"Yeah, well, I'm still at it."

"Do you ever hear from your ... "

"My mom?"

"Yeah."

"Nope."

The silence stretches between them. Cassie remembers clearly when Holden's mom left. That was around the time that she was accepted at St. Cat's. Actually, now that she thinks about it, that was when they broke up. They were only twelve, so it wasn't really a big deal, she reminds herself. Still, they had had something a bit deeper than most kids – they had in common their bad dreams.

They had in common the fact that they had no one else to talk to about what had happened.

They had in common what they had seen. They were the only one, except Matt. He was there, too. But somehow, it never seemed to bother him in the same way.

"Do you still have those dreams?" she asks, looking out the window.

"What dreams?"

"Forget it."

"No, wait. I do. I just ... "

"I know, I don't talk about it either." Her face takes on a haunted look. "Let's pretend I didn't say anything," she says.

"But ... "

"Forget it," she says. "I don't want to talk about it."

The silence stretches between them. They both think about the green water and the whales and the terrible look on the girl's face as she drowned. It fills the space between them.

It's probably why they had been such good friends,

why they had felt such a strong bond. Holden wants to ask her why she stopped writing to him, why she never called when she was in town visiting. She is so quiet and serious looking, he can't. He hardly knows her anymore. Does he? Is she still the same Cassie?

"So you go back tomorrow, huh," Holden says.

"Yup, first thing in the morning."

"So I guess this is goodbye."

"Will you miss me?" Cassie bats her eyelashes playfully, kidding around like she did when she was a goofy little kid, but Holden knows that he will. He will miss her. She's the only girl that he has dated that he ever really ... well. That he really liked a lot. He looks into her green eyes, flecked with yellow. Cat's eyes, he thinks. She pushes her hair behind her ear, looking around for a waiter to bring their bill.

"Yeah," he says so quietly that perhaps she doesn't hear. "I will."

They stare quietly out the window of the restaurant. The moon is reflecting off the ocean, leaving a scar of light across the calm surface.

"Please take the brochure, ma'am," Mark Mitchell says as nicely as possible. "It's just something to think about."

"Are there any coupons in here?"

"Coupons?"

"Yeah. For the gift shop or somethin'."

Mark smiles politely. "No, ma'am. It's just information."

"Well, I don't need no more paper than I already got," she says rudely.

She pushes by him with her three nasty-looking kids in tow. One of them turns around and gives him the finger.

Charming. He looks at his watch. It's only three o'clock and he is sick of this already. The California theme-park staff have tried to kick him off the property several times, so now he and his friends are standing as close to the parking-lot driveway as they can without actually crossing the property line. It's hot in the southern sun, not like October in Vancouver, that's for sure, and people aren't generally being very receptive to his brochure. What a way to spend his Thanksgiving vacation. His wife was angry that he left, too, what with the baby on the way in November. What if it comes early? she had asked.

He wears a beeper on his belt, just in case. If he gets paged, he'll go straight to the airport and get home, no matter how much it costs.

It's frustrating work, but he has a good cause, he reminds himself, thinking about the whales trapped in captivity, tortured by the boring routines they are forced to endure day in and day out, training practices that make the hair on the back of his neck stand to attention. It's his life's work, his and Todd's, although Todd is focusing his efforts on making all whaling illegal and lobbying government to outlaw whale watching. He thinks, and Mark agrees, that people should just start leaving the whales alone for once. Ever since one orca was accidentally trapped in a fisherman's net and became a tourist attraction, the industry has spiraled out of control. If they don't try to make change, who will?

"How do you know so much, smart ass?" one of the passersby asks.

"I used to work there," he says simply. "My brother was a trainer. We used to be part of the problem."

The man takes the leaflet, shrugging. "Okay, I'll take a look."

But still he pays his money and goes in, dropping the flier in the garbage just inside the gate. The girl in the ticket booth smirks at Mark and waves. The volume of people that have gone through the gates already today is staggering, and at twenty dollars per ticket, the theme park has already made more money today than Mark does in a month. No wonder things don't change, he thinks. Money is power.

One more day, and he has to be back at the school. Realizing this, he picks up his pace a little, pushing paper after paper into the hands of the tourists.

"Just read it," he insists. "Think about it."

FIVE

"Holden and Cassie, sittin' in a tree, K-I-S-S-I-N-G," sings Matt.

"Okay, okay, I deserve that," answers Holden, grinning madly. "All right already."

"... first comes love, then comes marriage, then comes Holden with the baby carriage ... "

"Very funny. You win."

"Holden and Cassie ... "

"That's enough!" Holden reaches over and punches Matt gently in the gut. "Shut up. Or I'll start about Taylor. Taylor says this, Taylor says that ... "

"Okay. Stop. Fine."

"Besides," adds Holden, "Cassie doesn't even know

that I like her in that way. I think ... maybe ... Taylor knows how you feel."

"All right, all right. Hey, you wanna get some pizza?"

"Sure. Your treat?"

"You're pathetic, did anyone ever tell you that? Moocher."

"Race you to the car, asshole."

Matt wins easily. He always does. Come to think of it, the only place Holden ever runs to is the bathroom when he has to puke. He's really going to stop drinking. This time, for real. Maybe he'll even join one of those groups. Maybe. Cassie wouldn't think very much of him if she knew he was a drunk, would she? He trips over his shoelace and stops to tie it, kneeling on the cold cement. By the time he gets to the car, he's completely out of breath. Matt's already sitting in the driver's seat, grinning insanely.

"What a loser," he laughs, shaking his head.

Holden grins back. "Just drive, my man. Just drive."

They wait in the little car while the defroster attacks the frozen windshield. Holden can feel his cheeks flushing in the hot air from the dash. Behind his closed eyelids he pictures Cassie, her head back, laughing in the moonlight. After they went out for dinner at the end of Thanksgiving break, they had gone for a long walk along the edge of the golf course that wound around a craggy bay. He had frightened her with stories of the ghost of a girl in a white dress that is said to haunt the Victoria Golf Club. He told the story so convincingly, he half believed he saw the ghost crouched down behind the bench on the point. He had jumped and she had laughed and laughed, and it had felt so right, like they were meant to be together. He had never felt so comfortable with anyone else, ever. It was their shared history, sure; they'd grown up on the same block and had played together ever since they were toddlers. But it was something more, as well, something better. He grins.

"What are you grinning at, monkey-boy?"

"Nothing, I was just...thinking."

"Yeah, right. I'm sure. Hey listen, me and Taylor are going to have a beach party for the first day of December, you know? You want to come?"

"The first day of December?" repeats Holden, dubiously. "Won't it be really cold?"

"Yeah, that's the point. That it's cold, but still not too cold to be outside. We'll have a fire and stuff. It'll be really cool."

"Okay, maybe. Whatever."

I won't be drinking by then, Holden promises himself. It will be the first party he goes to where he doesn't touch a drop. He stares out the window, pleased with himself. Already, it seems like he has a little bit less of a headache. Already, he feels healthier.

"It's not the real thing," Sina reminds her, as Cassie gnaws her nails to the quick. "Don't get so stressed out. You're still a month away from the big performance. Think of it as a dress rehearsal."

"I know, I know. I'm just tired, I guess."

"You look awful. I heard you get up last night. Bad dreams again?"

Cassie shrugs. "I guess."

"What do you dream about, anyway?"

"I ... I really ... I don't remember," she lies. "I don't know."

"Weird, huh?"

"Weird," Cassie agrees. She closes her eyes and leans back against the backstage wall. She doesn't want to talk, she just has to concentrate. In her head she counts her vertebrae, each one biting into the cold bricks. One, two, three ... She centers all her attention on focusing on each bone. This is the first time she will have performed 'Tourmente de Neige' in front of an audience. Okay, so it's not really an audience, it's just the little kids from the primary school. But still. She takes a breath.

"I'm okay now, Sina, really. Thanks for sitting with me. I'll be fine. I think I'm going to go do my stretches."

"You're sure you're all right?"

"Yes, ma'am. Really. Go sit in the audience. I'll survive, I promise."

She waits for Sina to get to her seat before she runs

into the tiny backstage bathroom to vomit. Her hands are shaking. I really have to get more rest, she thinks. I'm never going to make it if I keep this up. From the stage, she hears the distant chords of the piano. The acoustics are terrible. The notes ring out tinnily in the room. The chords change, become heavier. It's her cue – the show is starting.

She takes another deep breath, and holds it in tightly.

"Okay," she says to herself. "I'm okay."

She runs out to the stage entrance. Her muscles are ready; she can feel them trembling.

Then – she's on. As soon as her feet hit the stage, she's fine. The shivering stops. Her body flies through the air, every practiced step and twirl unfolds like magic. She looks up at the lights. *Demi-plié* to *chasée. Pas de chat, battement tendu. Arabesque, bourrée*. Steps flow through her mind like a road map. She follows the path created by the music, feels herself relaxing into the dance. She lets it go, lets it take her.

The little kids watch with awed expressions, dreaming of the day when they will be on the stage.

She stumbles once at the beginning of the piece. Sina watches her friend waver and shrugs. She has some sleeping pills she'll offer to her friend. Cassie's just tired, that's all.

All those nightmares, all those early-morning practices.

Someone else notices, too. In the back, Mark

Mitchell shakes his head. He'll call her parents, he decides. She needs to talk to someone. Maybe they'll agree to let him try to help. Maybe. After all, he did his undergrad biology degree with a minor in psychology. He knows a little bit about post-traumatic disorders. Not much, but a bit. And what she saw must have been awful. It must have been unimaginable.

He shudders and goosebumps fleck his skin.

Just at that moment, his pager buzzes. His pager! At first he doesn't know what it is, or what it means. He leaps from his seat and knocks over the plastic chair.

"Sorry," he whispers. "Excuse me."

The clatter makes Cassie hesitate again. This time, she stops mid-turn and steps heavily onto the stage. It's a big, noticeable mistake. There is no way she can cover it up. Idiot, she berates herself. She tries to get back into the rhythm again, but can't quite get back on track.

Damn Mr. Mitchell, she thinks. He's always messing things up. I'll practice more, she promises herself. She'll get up earlier every day and go through the whole routine a few times before breakfast. She only has a month, and it has to be perfect.

Cassie has to be perfect.

She doesn't know how else to be.

SIX

"Holden!"

Holden adjusts the volume on the stereo. It's just low enough that he can hear his father bellowing up the stairs.

"*Hol*den!"

He turns it up again until the throbbing of the bass vibrates the floorboards. He turns back to his painting. This is the first time he has tried to do one that doesn't involve the ocean, and he can't seem to get the colors right. The color of Cassie's hair, for example, is coming out too harsh. It's really much softer. A much gentler, but stronger red. Damn. If he could see her, it would help. He adds another drop of crimson to the palette.

It's also the first time he's tried to paint while he's sober.

"*Holden*!" his dad yells again.

"Dad. *What*? I'm *working* up here! What do you *want*?"

"Holden, get down here. I'm not going to ask again."

"Shit," swears Holden, placing the palette carefully on the table. The red was just about right, too. For good measure, he takes a long swig of Coke, belching ungraciously.

"I'm *coming!*"

He takes his time setting down the brush, dragging his feet on the narrow wooden stairs, swinging for a second from the top of the hall door.

When he walks into the kitchen, he knows immediately that something is wrong. He can tell instantaneously that he would rather be upstairs with Cassie-on-canvas and a beer than down here in this room. Shit. His father runs his hands through his thick grey hair once. Twice. He clears his throat. Loosens his tie.

"What is it, Dad? I'm trying to *work*."

"Holden."

"That's me."

"I have to ... We have to ... talk. About your mother."

"My mother?" Holden tries to keep the shock out of his voice. His dad has not mentioned his mother to him since she left. Not once.

"Yes. She's ... "

"Dad, what is it? She's dead? What is it? What the hell is it?"

His father stares out the window. Holden notices his hand shaking. His heart skips a beat, and the cola rises in his throat. Something must be wrong, something must really be wrong.

"Dad ... tell me."

"This is really hard to say, son."

"Dad!"

"She's coming home." The words fall from his lips like stones.

"She what? Dad? What?" Holden's lips are trembling. "She's coming home?"

"There's more," his dad says, sighing heavily.

"What more? That's great. I guess. I mean, where the hell has she been? Why does she think she can just waltz back in here again like there's noth – "

"*Holden*."

"What?"

"There's something ... Holden. She's not well. She ..."

"Dad, you're driving me crazy. What is it?"

"She has AIDS."

"She *what*?"

"She's an addict, Holden. She has a problem. Had a problem. Now she has a bigger problem."

Holden sits down with a thud on the hard kitchen chair. The pain in his butt makes him feel a little better.

"So she's coming home."

"Didn't you hear me, Holden? She's sick. She needs me now. Us. She needs us."

"Yeah. I heard you."

The house has had an empty echo in it since she left. Even now, he can hear their voices bouncing around the room. His mom is coming home. On the walls there are pictures lined up of Holden: grades one through seven. His dark hair slicked back by his mother's hand. His black-brown eyes squinting happily from the frames. In a couple of the pictures, he is missing teeth, and in the last one he is wearing braces. He would have been in seventh grade when she left; he was twelve when suddenly time in this house stood still, everything staying exactly as she left it. She didn't ever see him with the braces off his teeth. The only things that have changed, he reflects, are him and his father. His father aged about a hundred years, and Holden, well ... he got taller, anyway. Taller and drunker.

"Well, Dad," he says. "I guess things are going to be different around here."

"You can say that again, son," his father says, still staring out the window into the tangled garden. "You can say that again."

Back upstairs, Holden stares at the phone. He wishes he had a drink. Like mother, like son, he thinks fleetingly. What the hell. He goes back downstairs, steals a beer from the fridge and returns to his attic room. The bottle is cold and familiar, and the glass sweats in the heat of the radiator. He opens it carefully and downs it in three gulps, feeling the icy froth spread in his gut.

What he really needs is a shoulder to cry on. Fleetingly, he thinks of Cassie. Cassie, who is not his girlfriend. Cassie, who doesn't even live in the same city. The beer tastes stale in his mouth.

"You're an idiot," he tells himself aloud. His voice seems to echo in the huge space.

He picks up the phone and dials Matt's number.

"Hey, what's going on?" says Matt.

"Not much. Hey, Matt ... "

"Yeah?"

"You doing anything?"

"Yeah, actually. I am. I mean, I'm just on my way to Taylor's. We're going to hang out or something. Go for a run. You want to come? I'm sure it would be cool with her ... "

"Nah, forget it. When are you going?"

"Half an hour. What's up?"

"I just ... well. You know, my dad just ... "

"What? Spill it, buddy."

"Well, it's just ... apparently, my mom's coming home."

"Wow. Really?"

"Apparently."

"Isn't she, like, a druggie or something?"

Holden shrugs. "Not anymore," he says. "That's what Dad said. She's in recovery. But ... "

"But what?"

"Oh nothing. Forget it. Listen, you want to hang out tomorrow?"

"Sure, buddy. Listen, I've got to go."

"Later."

The dial tone hums in Holden's ear. I need another drink, he thinks, his heart beating too fast in his chest. I need a damn drink! Not caring about what his dad might say, he throws caution to the wind. He thuds downstairs. Blatantly opens the liquor cabinet and grabs the first thing his hand touches. Grand Marnier, he notices, as he makes his way back up to the attic. He sniffs it suspiciously. It smells awful. But it will do. It will do in an emergency.

He puts the canvas of Cassie aside, actually puts it in the furthest corner away, a dark spidery corner. Dust settles on the fresh paint. He pulls out an older canvas and stares at it in disgust.

"This is awful," he says to himself. "Terrible."

It needs more color. More green. More blue. More shadows. More contrast. Holden starts painting over the canvas with the picture that never leaves his head. The only thing he can really paint: black-and-white shadows through the filter of green winter light. He paints it through a glass window. He adds the back of three little kids' heads, looking up. Layer after layer. The picture becomes three dimensional, the oils forming heavy blobs on the old dry paint. He paints his way through the bottle. The sweet drink coats his teeth and his lips and the smell permeates everything.

When he finally passes out, he dreams of Cassie. Cassie at the beach, walking her dog. Cassie walking along the rocky shore. He's calling her, calling. The surf is getting bigger, but she doesn't seem to notice. Green-grey waves breaking over her legs. "Cassie!" In the rolling waves, he can see a familiar shape, lunging towards the shore, hidden in the green.

"Cassie!"

He wakes up shouting, sweat pouring down his brow. His gut churns. He turns over, feels the familiar, paint-spattered floor against his cheek. Oh no, he thinks, seeing the tipped bottle of Grand Marnier. He staggers to his feet, beating the now familiar path down the narrow stairs to the bathroom.

"Idiot," he whispers, as he drops to his knees in front of the toilet.

Can his father hear him retch? He hopes he can. He hopes he hears and feels bad about the way his son turned out.

Cassie shakes out another tiny white pill from the bottle that Sina gave her. These are great, she thinks. For the last two weeks, she has actually slept through the night. Her hands have trembled less, and she looks a little less pale, a little less gaunt. The pill tastes sweet on her tongue, as she swallows it dry. She listens to Mr. Mitchell drone on and on about micro-organisms in the ocean. Like this matters to any of them. Everyone in the class is an actress or a singer or a dancer. Or something. None of us care, she thinks, glaring at the teacher. She projects her thoughts as loudly as she can. Don't care, she thinks. Be quiet.

"Do you have something to add, Cassie?"

"Um, no."

"Care to answer my last question?"

"Oh, um, no. Sorry. Actually, I sort of ... " She sighs. "I wasn't listening, okay?"

"Not okay, Cassie. See me after class, please."

Great, she thinks, staring out the window into the deserted quad. Now I'll be late for rehearsal.

Sina rolls her eyes sympathetically, but Cassie looks away. She is so tired. She puts her head down on her desk, lets Mr. Mitchell's droning voice put her to sleep.

"Cassie! Cassie! Wake up!"

"Wha – ?"

"You know, Cassie, I am angry that you don't pay attention in class. But I'm also worried about you. First, you never sleep. Now, I see you taking pills in class, and you sleep on your desk. What's going on?"

"Nothing," she shrugs, looking past him to the empty classroom. "Just tired, I guess."

"Cassie, you can talk to me, you know. If you need someone to talk to."

"Gee, thanks, Mr. Mitchell. I'll keep it in mind. Look, I'm sorry I wasn't concentrating. I have a big show coming up, I guess I'm distracted. Can you just give me some kind of lines to write or something? I'm late for rehearsal."

Mark frowns. "Go ahead," he tells Cassie. "Just do me one favor?"

"What?"

"Give me the pills."

"Or else?"

"Or else I'll have to report you."

"Fine." Cassie fights the tears welling up behind her eyes. Blinks them back. "Here," she says, tossing him the bottle. "Thanks a lot."

"Goodbye, Cassie."

She runs out the door, down the endless corridor to rehearsal. She'll be in trouble if she's too late. And what is she going to do without the pills?

Red hair flying, she bursts into the studio, hands reaching up to twist and knot her unruly locks into submission, into a ballerina's controlled tight bun.

That evening, down at the Dallas Road beach, Matt and Taylor have the music on their boom box cranked up as loud as they dare. Holden watches them through the flickering fire. There are no houses overlooking this barren part of the shore, and it is completely dark except for the dancing light of the flames. The trees lean low over the water, providing a ceiling between them and the immeasurable sky. The waves lap gently and unthreateningly on the shore. Holden chugs back a beer and drops down on his back in the cold, damp sand and stares at the canopy of stars through the cloud of his own breath.

"It's freezing," he says. "This is absurd."

Matt and Taylor don't bother answering because they are busy making out on the blanket. Great, thinks Holden. Talk about being a third wheel. He throws the empty beer bottle into the undergrowth and hears it break on a rock. The crash is strangely satisfying. He closes his eyes and listens to the music and tries to block out Matt and Taylor.

It's so dark on the beach, and so private under these trees. The smoke from the fire stings their eyes, but keeps them warm. Sparks hover in the night.

"Matt?"

"Oh, sorry – too much, huh?"

"No ..."

Holden listens to the sound of them kissing and groping. Shut it out, he tells himself. Don't listen. Jesus.

He can hear them breathing heavily.

"Matt?" Taylor whispers.

"Yeah?"

"Is he asleep?"

"Passed out, I think," Matt whispers.

I can hear you, Holden wants to say, but he doesn't. What the hell. He can't be bothered. Let them have their fun.

"You know what we could do," Matt suggests.

"What?"

"We could do this!" He leaps to his feet suddenly and moves out of the light from the fire. Holden hears the rustling sound of clothes being removed. Yuck, he thinks. Too late now – he'll have to pretend to be completely unconscious. How embarrassing.

"Hey, what are you doing?" he hears Taylor ask.

A sweater appears on the blanket next to him. A pair of jeans. Socks.

Jesus, he's getting naked. Holden can't believe this is happening.

"Matt?" he hears Taylor say. "Matt? What are you – "

Then he hears the splash. His heart thuds crazily in his chest. Matt's crazy. He sits up. He can't even see his friend in the dark water.

"Matt? Where the hell did you go?"

A cold sweat breaks out on Holden's brow.

"Taylor!! Come on," he hears Matt say. "The water's great! It's warm!"

"Sure. It's not like it's December or anything. Oh, wait, yes it is," he hears her reply.

"Come on ... "

"Forget it."

"Come on, Taylor ... I thought this is what you wanted ... "

"No way. I mean it, Matt. Quit fooling around."

"Yeah, Matt, you asshole," adds Holden.

"Holden?"

"Get out of the water, you creep."

"Come on in, the water's great!"

"Jerk." He turns his back on Matt. In the light of the fire, he can see that Taylor looks really pissed off. Who can blame her? he wonders. What a night.

He kicks a pile of wet sand over the fire. It hisses and sizzles. So much for the evening. He stuffs the last few bites of potato salad in his mouth and puts the container away. He drinks the last of the wine. Taylor doesn't look like she wants any more, that's for sure.

"Come on, Matt. We're leaving. You'll freeze to death if you stay in much longer."

"No, I won't!"

He can hear the splashing as Matt's muscular arms stroke through the gentle waves. By the light of the moon, he can see his blonde hair. He has swum out a hundred feet, or more.

"Come back," Holden says, his voice cracking. "Don't go out so deep."

"What? I can't hear you!" Matt dives down with a kick of his feet, disappears from sight.

Sweat drips down Holden's face. His hands are trembling.

"God damn you, Matt," he whispers under his breath. "Get in here right now."

"It's not him that's afraid," Taylor reminds him quietly. "It's not his problem."

"Yeah? Well, he's not my problem either."

Holden storms away as well as he can. He trips a couple of times on logs and driftwood. He can hear Matt and Taylor talking. The idiot must have got out of the water. Jerk. Now Holden feels stupid about the whole thing. Maybe he overreacted. He was acting like it was a scene from *Jaws*. Taylor's right. It's not Matt's problem, it's his.

Everything is his problem.

He kicks the sand angrily. The night air is freezing and the steps are slippery with frost as he makes his way up to the street. Luckily, he is still a bit drunk. That keeps the chill off, a bit. Just enough to get him home.

SEVEN

"Holden, are you listening to me?"

"Yes, Dad, what do you want?"

"Holden, I wish you would be a little more polite."

"Fine, Dad."

"Holden, I don't know how long this is going to take."

"Why? I thought you said she wanted to come home."

"Not exactly. But she did call to say she was sick. I think what she meant was ... "

"Dad, are you serious? You're going all the way to Los Angeles and you don't even know if she wants to see you?"

"I'll talk her into it," his dad says quietly. "I think

she wants to come."

"You're being awfully nice to her considering she's a junkie and she left you," Holden mumbles.

"What's that? What did you say?"

"Nothing, Dad," he sighs. "Forget it. I just said you were being awfully nice to do this."

"Hmm. I've left some money for you in the usual place. For groceries. I mean it, Holden. Not for liquor, you understand me? Keep your receipts."

"Yes, Dad. Fine."

His dad reaches out to him, and for a split second Holden thinks he is going to hug him or something weird. Instead, he rests his hand on Holden's shoulder and pats him awkwardly. Holden shrugs and steps away.

"Bye, Dad," he says, and turns his back.

The emptiness of the house reverberates when his father slams the front door behind him. Dust seems to lift off every surface and hover in the air, for just a second, before settling back down again. He's left alone. For a few days, weeks? Who knows how long. There is a cookie jar full of money in the kitchen.

He goes and grabs the cash and stuffs it in his pocket. He grabs his bike. He'll be able to buy some more canvases. He's been painting over old ones and he's almost run out of those. This is perfect timing. Maybe he'll get a new brush, too, as an early Christmas present to himself. Thanks, Dad, he says to himself. Thanks a lot.

He might even score some pot. This time he has really quit drinking. Not a drop, he promises. But maybe some pot to take the edge off his nerves.

He pedals hard into the December wind. Tries not to think about what it will be like to have his mom home. His sick mom. His dying mom. He pushes the thought out of his head and pedals faster and harder. Ice-cold air fills his lungs. Finally, he feels his headache begin to recede.

Maybe he'll paint a picture for her, he thinks to himself. Maybe she'll want to see how he didn't stop just because she left. How he just kept going in spite of her.

Maybe he won't, though. Maybe he doesn't want to give her the satisfaction.

By the time he gets home, it's almost dark. The house is so empty it reverberates with stillness. He thinks about cleaning it, but changes his mind. His footsteps seem to echo in the void. My mom is coming home, he says to himself experimentally. Maybe he will have one drink. Just one. He'll start fresh tomorrow, no drinks.

The new supplies fill his backpack, and he can hardly wait to get upstairs and unpack them. He should eat first, he thinks, turning on the light in the kitchen. He is deciding whether or not to open a can of soup when the phone rings.

"Hey," Matt says. "Guess who I saw on TV?"

"Dunno. Who?" Holden takes a swig of pear brandy. It's the only thing left in the liquor cabinet and it tastes awful, but good at the same time. This is the last thing I'll ever drink, he promises himself.

"Miss Cassidy Wagner herself."

"Who?" says Holden, who wasn't really paying attention. "What?"

"Cassie, you idiot."

"Really?"

"Yeah, some ballet thing. She's in some big show at the Queen Elizabeth in Vancouver next week."

"Really?"

"Stop saying that. Yeah, really."

"She's in a show? Hey, I think she told me about this ... something about snow?"

"I dunno. It just said it was something to do with that school she goes to. Anyway, it's at the Queen Elizabeth, so it must be some big-deal thing."

"Wow," says Holden, genuinely impressed.

"Yeah, wow."

"How'd she look?"

"Same. We just saw her, remember?"

"I know, I just ... hey!"

"What?"

"You want to go to the show?"

"Go?"

"To see the show. With me."

"How?"

"It'll be cool. Come on." The idea forms in Holden's head as he speaks. He thinks of the money in the cookie jar. There's still a bit there, even after he bought the supplies. All those lessons in thriftiness must have paid off. "I'll pay," he adds. "My dad left me some cash."

"Yeah? Where did he go?"

"Oh, he had to go to California, to get ... well. He's gone for, like, a while. I don't know. He might be back next week, but I don't know."

"Okay. Yeah. Let's do it. Whoooeeee!"

Holden pours the rest of the brandy down the sink. It clings to the chrome and leaves a sticky path. No more, he says. This time for real.

From her prone position backstage, Cassie can see the top of the curtain, the wires that suspend the lights above the stage, and the carved tiles. Breathe, she reminds herself. Breathe.

The theater is dark and cool and silent. In the stillness, she can feel her own heart beating, a tiny bird fluttering in her chest. The band of fear tightens.

"I'm going to be sick," she whispers to no one in particular.

"No, you're not," she hears floating back to her in the darkness. The disembodied voice is soothing. She closes her eyes.

Last night she dreamt that she looked out into the audience and it was gone. It had turned into the ocean. Endless green ocean. She was dancing on a stage, and all around was water, and in the water was her nightmare. Slapping tails splashed her while she danced and danced and danced. She knew all the while that the whales would lure her into the water, knew that she would be pulled down. She wishes she had those pills. They kept the dreams down, muted her sleep into nothingness.

She stretches, feeling the wooden stage digging into her bare back. All the tense muscles in her shoulders seem to sigh. Breathe, she tells herself again. You'll be fine.

In the shadows, she slowly makes her way onto her mark. The stage is huge. Much bigger than she remembers it from rehearsal. In the audience someone coughs. She thinks she hears a baby whimpering. Who would bring a baby to a performance? she thinks angrily. There are whispers, and programs rustling. She bites her lip nervously. The burgundy velvet curtain rises and light floods her eyes. She can't see. Somewhere, way in the distance, over the sound of her own breathing, she can hear the music. She knows she should start moving, but she is paralyzed. How long does she stand there? The music gets louder.

Now, she thinks, now.

Slowly, her body unfurls, rising towards the lights. In that split second, she steps outside herself and lets go. She twirls and twirls across the stage, aware of all the bones in her spine, twisting together. The muscles in her legs bunching and releasing, throwing her through the air.

Cassie dances. And dances.

Before she knows it, it's over. She's backstage, sweaty and tired. She can hardly believe twenty minutes have passed. She catches sight of Madame, who grins and winks, giving her the thumbs up.

She stands behind the curtain offstage where she can see the other dancers. It's so beautiful, she thinks. They all look so beautiful. Even the littlest girls, dressed as snowflakes, doing clumsy *pliés* in a crooked line.

She scans the audience for familiar faces. She knows her parents won't be there. Her dad is in Arizona at a flaky shrink conference, and her mom didn't want to leave Xav at home alone. Or, heaven forbid, with a sitter. In the front, she can see Sina and her mom clapping like mad.

The lights are playing tricks with her eyes. It's hard to see into the audience. Mostly, it's a sea of black. But there, in the third row. Is it? She squints. The two faces look familiar. If the light were a little better ... She could swear that she sees Matt and Holden, whispering behind a folded program.

Holden? Her heart skips a beat. A flush creeps over her sweaty cheeks. Would he have come all the way over here to see her?

But when the lights come up, those seats are empty. She curtsies and curtsies, staring at the vacant chairs.

The applause goes on and on. She smiles. This is all she's ever wanted.

"Cassie! Cassie, come here!" Madame Chantelle beckons to her backstage.

"Yes, Madame?"

"Cassie, while you were dancing, these came for you," Madame says with a twinkle in her eye.

She reaches behind the piano and pulls out a bouquet of peach-colored roses.

"They're beautiful," she breathes. "From my parents?"

"Oh, I don't know. Maybe you should read the card."

Congratulations, Holden

Madame's eyes sparkle. "New boyfriend, Cassie?"

"No," she shrugs, hiding the writing. "From my parents, after all."

Liar, she thinks, cradling the flowers. Why would she lie? The flowers are beautiful and the scent is thick and sweet. Holden. She smiles. She'll call him when she gets home at Christmas. Maybe, there's something there.

It is nice to have a friend from the past, she thinks, someone who isn't all caught up in dancing or acting or competing for parts. Someone who remembers what she was like when she was a kid. Holden. He is sweet, he's a good friend, *and* he came all this way to see me dance.

And he's pretty good-looking. She grins at herself in the mirror and unpins her hair. He sure is cute.

Mark looks out the window of the plane. The night sky looks cold and dark. Miles below is the ocean, teeming with life. He pictures the whales on their migratory routes, passing unnoticed below them, their huge bodies moving slowly in their own graceful ballet. He wonders if they know of all the fuss that goes on about them on the land. Probably not, he muses. That's what makes them so special. Their ability to be oblivious to us, to people, the most obnoxious species on the planet. He shivers. It's cold on the plane, and at takeoff the pilot announced that it was snowing heavily in Tokyo and that that might cause delays. It makes Mark colder just to think about it. What a way to spend Christmas, he thinks. Especially his son's first Christmas. His wife sighs in her sleep and adjusts her position on his shoulder, the baby bundled tightly to her chest. If it's important to you, she had said, it's important to me, too. Someone has to do it.

You're right, he had agreed. Now he wonders. Sometimes he gets tired, working all the time, and now he's dragging his wife and new baby along. He is starting to question his priorities. They'll stay at the hotel, he reassures himself. They'll have time to relax. He, on the other hand, has much to do. He is meeting with the Japanese chapter of his anti-captivity group and then they are going to distribute his new literature at three major aquariums. A TV station has promised them time to pitch their new video as well. His wife will stay in Tokyo, and he will have to travel by bus to each of three locations.

He remembers the whales and tries to push past his fatigue. Unfortunately for the whales, they are currently very popular in Japan. Not as popular as in America, of course. Not yet. But it's just a matter of time. He clears his throat, mentally prepares his lecture. His well-rehearsed anti-captivity speech. It's so obvious, really, he doesn't know how his brother could ever have got involved with the other side, ever been a trainer who used such obviously cruel techniques to force the whales to jump through hoops day after day.

Whales rely very heavily on sonic waves. Imagine being in a concrete pool, all that sound bouncing around and around. Trapped in a little puddle, when you were made to travel fifty, sixty, a hundred miles per day. He shudders.

Someone has to try and make it stop. Even if it means giving up a Christmas holiday. He leans back in his seat and lowers his tray. Time to get to work.

He takes some pamphlets out of his bag and starts reading. He needs to have these facts at his fingertips. Soon, his eyes get heavy. He is lulled to sleep by the roar of the plane engine and his wife's deep, even breathing and the damp breaths of the baby. In his dream he gives speeches. He throws the pamphlets in the air and they rain down on the city like snowfall, spreading in drifts along the streets.

EIGHT

Cassie shifts uncomfortably on the church pew. It's the day before Christmas Eve, and she has just arrived home with barely enough time to put down her bag before being dragged out again to the church to see the annual Christmas pageant. Her last performance was last night and her head is still spinning. She can feel her bones bumping into the uncushioned wood. Beside her, her mom and dad fidget with their prayer books.

"What's the matter?" she hisses to her mother.

"Oh," says her mom, "I'm just nervous for your brother. Isn't this exciting?"

"Yeah," she mumbles. "Really." Exciting? This? Her brother, Xav, is in some stupid Christmas play. He doesn't even have a real part; he's just a shepherd boy or something. Why would her mother be nervous? It's not like she's ever bothered to come and see Cassie perform, and she had a lead role! She was on TV!

Just because Xav has some disabilities, they have to make him feel special. Doesn't she get to be special, too?

"Stop moving around, Cassie," says her father sharply.

"I can't help it. These seats are totally uncomfortable."

"Perhaps you should eat more," her mother whispers. "Stop starving yourself to death."

"Me? Great. Sure, Mom."

Cassie never diets; she just dances and exercises and maybe she's just lucky. It's her mom who's always on the diet, nibbling on raw green leaves and plain rice. She rolls her eyes, wishing Sina were here to talk to. She holds her breath experimentally. Maybe she can make herself faint and get out of here. Wait till her parents see that.

"Stop it, you two," says her dad, leaning over. "It's starting!"

Oh, big excitement, thinks Cassie, glaring at the makeshift stage. Big deal. She imagines herself getting up out of the pew, shedding her uncomfortable shoes, stepping onto the stage. She smiles, starting to enjoy herself. The choir starts singing softly, and Cassie closes her eyes and pictures herself dancing on the tiny stage.

Jeté, balancé, arabesque. Her gossamer skirt flows like water around her legs. *Brisé volé, fouetté en tournant*. She can feel the dance moving inside her.

When she finally opens her eyes, she realizes the play is over.

Her parents are standing.

"Honestly, Cassie," her mother snipes. "Falling asleep is a little rude. Imagine how hurt your brother must feel."

What about me? she wants to scream. What about me?

But she stays quiet, watching herself pirouette across the now empty stage. One day, she thinks, one day they'll see.

Christmas Eve morning dawns bright and sunny. The sky is clear as far as the eye can see. In the living room Cassie can hear her father and Xav singing.

"I'm dreaming of a GREEN Christmas! Just like the one I always have!"

She wishes that it would snow. It used to snow at Christmas; she remembers it when she was a kid. The weather is so strange now. El Niño, or La Niña, or whatever it is. It's cold, really cold. But so clear. The ice sparkles on the window like a prism. A tiny rainbow of light appears on the ceiling.

The Wagners always start celebrating Christmas on Christmas Eve. Her mom says it's European, something she has always seemed to yearn to be. Whatever, Cassie thinks. It just means an extra day of presents.

She lies in bed, frowning. She was dreaming again. Only this time, it wasn't her in the water, it was Max. Max out chasing a stick at the beach. Max, swimming towards her, big eyes watching her. Max, not looking behind him, not seeing the black fin rising out of the water, not seeming to notice the teeth closing around him.

She cringes. Max. Where is he? He always sleeps with her. She sighs. Even Max is rejecting her. He's probably forgotten all about her. He probably even sleeps with Xav now. She pulls the blankets over her head. The sheets are decorated with tiny ballerinas, the sheets she has had on her bed forever. Her parents must think she is still eight years old, for God's sake. The pink tutus are visible from under the blanket. She groans. No escape.

"Cassie! Cassie! Get up! It's Christmas Eve!" Xav yells, flying into the room and landing on her bed with a crash, spilling over to the floor on the other side.

"I'm coming, I'm coming. Get off me, Xav. You're hurting me."

He flies out of the room like a tornado.

Great, she thinks. Two more weeks of this?

Downstairs, she looks around for Max. She has his reindeer antlers, which they always tie to his big old head for Christmas.

"Here, Max! Max, come! Max!"

In the kitchen she can hear pots and pans banging together over the sound of singing. Xav is yelling something about pancakes, while her parents do their best impression of holiday cheer. Her mom is trying to shape the pancakes like snowmen while her dad whips up omelets and hash browns and Xavier shouts and shrieks and giggles.

"Max!"

"Hey, Mom," she says. "Where's Max?"

The kitchen falls silent.

"Uh-oh," says Xav.

He darts out of the room, clutching his stocking to hang by the fireplace.

"Oh, Cassie," her mother sighs. "You had to bring that up? You know it upsets your brother."

"What upsets my brother?" says Cassie, confused. Her pulse quickens in her throat. "What are you talking about? What do you mean?"

"We had him put down. Right after Thanksgiving. He was so old, Cassie. He was tired."

"You had him put down? Because he was *tired*? You didn't *tell* me?"

"Well, we didn't want to upset you. You had so much schoolwork. And dancing. And we knew you were having a hard time. I guess we thought it would be best if we didn't tell you."

"You *killed* Max? And you didn't want to *disturb* me? You people," she says, staring daggers into them, "are totally fucking insane."

"Cassie," her father says in a warning tone, "don't spoil Christmas."

"Me? You don't want *me* to spoil Christmas? You've got to be kidding. Besides, it isn't even Christmas until *tomorrow*! Can't we even try to be normal for once?" She stares at them in disbelief. "I hate you," she adds under her breath. "I hate you both."

She runs upstairs, stumbling. Blinded by tears. Max was her dog, hers! They had no right to kill her dog. Because he was *old*? Blindly, she struggles into her jeans and a sweater, not bothering to brush her hair or wash up. She runs down the stairs and out into the cold morning, ignoring the slippery sidewalk. Inside her boots, her sockless feet wince against the cold cement. She shivers in the chill.

Don't spoil Christmas?

Tears stream down her cheeks. It's so cold, she imagines them freezing there against her skin, icicles of mourning.

"I'm tired, too," she shouts back at the house. "Are you going to have me put down?"

Where is she going to go? It's too cold to stay outside, and she can hardly go back home. The grass crunches with each step, each blade sheathed in a layer of frost. Her breath hangs in front of her, frozen. She half expects it to stay there, a permanent ice-cloud in front of her reddening nose. The sidewalk is slippery. She steps carefully; she can't risk injury, after all.

Holden. He's about the only person here who cares about her; he's about the only friend she's got. She half-walks, half-jogs towards his house, staying on lawns as much as she can to avoid any hidden patches of ice.

It's still early.

Holden is still sleeping up in the attic room, the empty bottle of vodka beside him. What's that sound? He closes his eyes again, reminding himself that the house is empty. Merry almost-Christmas, he says, lifting the bottle to his lips and throwing it aside with disgust when he realizes that it's empty. He's changed his mind about not drinking. What's Christmas without a couple of drinks? It's going to be his New Year's resolution, though. This time for real. Christmas is just too ...

He put up a Christmas tree this year in case his mom and dad got home before the holiday, but apparently they aren't going to show. That's okay. It's not like he bothered to decorate it or anything. His father called three days ago and said they were on their way. So where were they now? His head pounds. All these years, and he didn't know where she was. She didn't come looking for him, either. All that time.

His dad probably knew the whole time. All those

business trips were probably thinly disguised visits to her. They've probably just been hanging out in California, thinking how clever they were to leave him behind. Maybe not. But still.

The tree is sitting there in the living room, half dead. Holden forgot to water it. Needles are dropping all over the carpet in a dry shower of scent.

Cassie can see the yellowing Christmas tree through the window. It looks crooked, as though in addition to not watering it, they have forgotten to tighten the stand. Which they probably have, she reminds herself. Two men living alone. She rings the bell and listens to it ring hollowly through the house. No one answers.

"Holden?" she calls. "Are you here?"

Holden sits up. He could almost have sworn he heard a woman's voice calling his name.

"Mom?" he calls.

"Holden!"

"Who's there?"

"It's me, um, Cassie."

"Cassie? What are you doing here?"

"Holden, can you just come down?"

"I'm upstairs," he yells. "In the attic."

Cassie stands in the front hall, uncertain. She probably shouldn't have come. One look in the dusty mirror confirms her suspicions. Her hair is puffed up around her head in a giant afro, and there are violent red streaks from her tears on her face. She looks ridiculous. The dust makes her sneeze; she traces her name into the layer of grey on the table. It's been a long time since she has been in this house. Five years. She used to come over all the time, but that was only until they were in seventh grade. A lot has changed since then, since Holden's mom left. Sometimes she wishes she could go back to that time, to the years before she moved to Vancouver and changed schools and lost touch with Holden and everyone from her past. Before she lost touch with herself.

"Cassie?"

She jumps. "Oh, Holden. Hi. I'm sorry. Gosh, I woke you up. Right? I'll come back. I mean, I came by to say thanks for the roses. I was really surprised. I kept meaning to call, but I ... "

"What's the matter?"

She bursts into tears. "I'm sorry, I'm just ... My parents, they ... "

"What happened? Are they all right?"

"They killed Max! They had him put to sleep!"

"Your dog?"

"Yes!"

"Oh, Cassie. I'm sorry."

"You know what's worse?" she says.

"What?"

"I didn't notice! I didn't notice yesterday when I

got home! I didn't even notice he wasn't there!"

He puts his arms around her, horribly aware of the thin pajamas that separate them and of how he must stink like alcohol. Her shoulders heave.

"It's okay. Sshhhh."

He pats her back in a way he hopes is comforting.

"Listen, why don't you come upstairs? I should, you know, put some clothes on."

"Oh! Sure, of course. You must think I'm crazy, bursting in here on Christmas Eve like this ... I'm sorry." She laughs nervously.

"Stop apologizing! I'm glad you came. Besides," he gestures towards the living room, "Christmas isn't much of a holiday around here, as you can tell."

While Holden changes, Cassie waits in the studio in the attic. The window has no curtains, and from there she can see all the way to the ocean. Her breath steams up the glass. Through the patch she clears, she can see the school they went to when they were kids, she can see the roof of her own house, sparkling with frost in the sunlight.

"Hey," she says, when he comes into the room. "You can see Matt's house from here!"

"Yeah, I know. It's great, actually. You can see everything. Can see your house, too."

"Right. The dog-killer's house, you mean."

"Cassie, I'm sorry about your dog. That's really rough."

"Thanks. Hey, d'you have anything to drink around here?"

"I didn't think that you, you know ... With your dancing and stuff, I figured you didn't drink."

"I don't," she smiles wryly, "but it seems like the way to start celebrating Christmas."

"Okay, sure. If you want ... I'll see what I can do."

Ten minutes later, he reappears at the top of the stairs, bearing an ancient bottle of wine and two mugs.

"Jackpot," he says. "Found it in the basement."

The wine is thick and red and pungent. Holden's fingers leave clean prints on the dusty bottle.

"Cheers." She lifts her mug, clinking it against his.

"Yeah, Merry Christmas."

After one mugful, Cassie is gooned. She leans back on the sofa.

"Wow," she says. "I think that's enough for me."

"Are you okay?"

"Great. I can just tell it's enough, you know? Especially first thing in the morning."

Holden nods, though he doesn't. For Holden, there is never enough. Surreptitiously he fills his mug again. "Sure. You want me to get you some coffee?"

"No, not yet. Let's just sit here."

"Okay."

"Can I look at your paintings?"

"No! I mean. Sure. Go ahead."

"Are you sure?"

"I guess. No, I want you to. You can look at my paintings if you ... dance for me."

"Here?" She looks around dubiously at the plywood floor covered with paint spatters.

"Yeah, here. Why not?"

She shrugs. Her head is spinning from the wine. "Okay, why not. What shall I do?"

"I don't know. Some ballet stuff."

"Okay, let me think for a minute."

She unties her boots, feeling the rough wood under her bare feet.

"Don't look at my ugly feet," she says self-consciously.

She crouches down. She holds her breath, eyes closed, and listens to the beating of her heart, the sound of her breathing. She waits for the silent music to start in her head. Waits for the beat.

Holden watches as she dances. Her eyes are focused way past him, off in the distance. Her body is amazing, bending and blowing as if in a powerful wind. She dances and dances, the plywood floor thumping gently as she jumps and whirls.

He takes a sip of wine and chokes. His cough echoes in the huge space.

She stops dancing abruptly.

"What's the matter?" Holden asks.

"Oh, I ... I've never done that in front of anyone before. It's sort of a private dance. I'm sorry, I guess I kind of forgot you were there."

"It was beautiful. Really. It was great."

"It was nothing. I feel really stupid now. Must be the wine. Maybe I'll take that cup of coffee after all."

"Sure, no problem. I'll be right back."

"Hey!" she calls after him.

"Yeah?" he says, turning at the doorway to the stairs.

"What about your paintings?" she asks.

"Oh, they're all over there against the wall – go ahead and look. I'll be right back," Holden says, disappearing down the narrow stairs.

Cassie lifts the sheet covering the stacks of canvases and gasps. There, unfolding in vivid dark colors, are all her nightmares. She feels sick. The room tilts. Oh. So many canvases, covered with thick dark-green paint, covered with her dream water.

Holden hurries up the stairs with the coffee. He is still thinking about how amazing the dance was when he sees her huddled on the couch.

"Cassie? What's the matter?"

"Your paintings ... " she says, stunned.

"Yeah?"

"They just ... I don't know. I try not to think about that day, you know?" Her voice trembles.

"Oh."

"I still dream about it. Do you? Every night, I dream about it."

"Oh, Cassie," he sighs. "I didn't think they'd upset you. I guess they're just my way of dreaming about it, too. I'm sorry."

"Don't be. They're good, I guess. I mean, they are. Good. I was just surprised. Maybe a little shocked. I forget, sometimes, that I wasn't the only one there."

"I know what you mean."

"Has Matt seen them?"

"No! I mean, no. He's glanced at them, I guess. He's been here. He's just not into painting and stuff. If it's not a sport, he doesn't get it. You know. And I guess I thought he might think it was kind of weird. You know what he can be like."

"No, not really. I mean, I know him from when we were kids, but he's different now."

"Yeah. I guess we all are."

"I guess so."

Cassie takes a big gulp of her coffee and wrinkles her nose. "Yeesh! Did you make it yourself?"

"Strong?"

"You can say that again!"

"Want some more milk in it?"

"No, it's okay. It's good," she lies.

"You're a really good dancer, you know. You could be a professional. You're that good."

"Thanks. I'm glad you think so."

"I do, really."

"I hope you're right. I have an audition...if I tell you this, promise you won't tell? I didn't tell my parents."

"Sure."

"I have an audition for an important ballet company in Toronto. It's coming up in June."

"Toronto?" Holden swallows. Toronto. He'll never see her if she goes to Toronto. She may as well be on the moon. He stares out the window, not saying anything.

"I know – wild, huh?" says Cassie, not bothering to hide her excitement.

"Wow. That's great. Toronto." Holden tries to sound pleased.

They lean back and she savors the rich, bitter coffee taste and the heat of the mug in her hands. Glancing around, she notices something amongst the paintings leaning up against the wall in the corner.

"Hey, what's that one?"

"Which one?"

Surrounded by all the dark blue and green, she points to the flash of red and orange. "That one, at the back."

"Oh, that's ... nothing. Don't look at that one."

"No, I want to. Let me."

"No! I mean it. Don't." He tries to grab her arm, but she's too quick for him, dancing out of his grasp. Going over to the pile, she extracts the canvas.

"Oh my God," she says, staring down at the picture

of herself. Her red hair. Her skin. All that skin.

In the painting, she's not wearing any clothes. He has painted her likeness completely naked, like a Playboy centerfold.

"Oh my God, Holden," she whispers.

She had been remembering their friendship so fondly! She had been missing him as a friend! And here he was, imagining her naked. She feels totally violated, like he has reached over and taken off her clothes. She drops her coffee on the floor. The dark brown liquid seeps into the boards and disappears into the paint stains.

She runs down the stairs and out into the cold for the second time that day, her boots clutched in her shaking hand.

"Cassie, wait! Come back!" Holden yells.

She hears him, but she doesn't turn around. Why does everything have to change? Why do people have to change? she thinks. Why can't everything just stay the same?

NINE

Holden is dreaming.

He is diving with Matt, who has taken up the hobby with a vengeance. In Holden's dream, he bobs along in the current. A flash of silver to the right looks like it might be a fish. He kicks out to the side to go look – why wait around here with these pathetic fools? He flips over a couple of times experimentally. It feels okay, he thinks. It feels pretty good.

He isn't frightened at all, and then ... then he looks up at the surface and his dream becomes a nightmare. Bile rises in his throat. A dark shadow is blocking out the sun. In one brief second he is carried back to the Seaquarium and the dreams he can muffle only with drinks.

Whales!

He chokes for a minute, can't remember what to do. He has to get to the surface. He has to wake up. Desperately, he tries to even out his breathing. He can't breathe! The regulator needs to be cleared, but he can't remember how. He wasn't paying attention! He grabs the mouthpiece and pulls it away from his mouth, struggles out of the straps and drops his tank. Water gushes into the mask as he tries to kick towards the surface. Close to the reef, there is a huge bed of kelp. He is flailing and reaching, but his feet are caught in the kelp and he can't move. Through the murky water in his dream mask, he watches his tank sinking down into the weeds. It seems to take forever. He is braced for the impact of the whale's jaws. He can't breathe. The shadow looms over him.

Just as he is about to take in a lungful of water, Matt appears from nowhere, gesturing wildly. He takes the regulator out of his own mouth and passes it to Holden. Holden grabs it and takes a big breath, then passes it back. He points at the shadow. Matt looks up, seemingly unconcerned. He takes another breath, then dives down and untangles Holden's foot. Slowly, they rise to the surface, sharing the tank.

Closer to the shadow. Then closer. To his horror and humiliation and ultimate relief, Holden realizes that he was looking at the bottom of the boat.

He awakens with a start.

Great, now even in his *dream* he is embarrassing himself. He has fallen asleep on the couch again and the attic room smells strongly of paint and stale booze. Now that the school's final term has started, the teachers seem to be doling out homework like it's a lost art. His last term of his last year of school. Well, finally. So he is supposed to be doing an English assignment. He is trying to read some Shakespeare play. Boring. He can't concentrate with all those *wherefore's* and *thee's* cluttering up the talk. He hates school; he's flunking anyway, so what difference does it make?

Downstairs, he can hear the sound of his parents talking. It sounds foreign and unsettling. He wasn't really prepared to see his mom when they pulled up in the driveway on Christmas morning. He wasn't really prepared to see anyone, in all honesty, but particularly not her. It had all happened in slow motion. He had heard the car coming and had gone down to the door. He wasn't sure how he should act – cool and nonchalant? Happy? Angry? He had opened the door and watched as his dad helped her out, his expression kind and gentle. Not looking anything like he usually did, cold and businesslike or mad and yelling. His mom had stepped out of the car like some kind of fragile princess. She was really thin; he was shocked by how thin she was. He felt about a million feelings all at once. She walked towards him really slowly and he looked at her and his heart was beating like crazy and he could feel himself starting to cry. She looked so small and vulnerable, but at the same time tough and aged. She's thirty-seven, he thought to himself. She looks fifty-five. She had reached out and taken his hand and shaken it quite formally.

"Hi," she said.

"Hi," he answered stiffly.

Neither one of them knew what to say then, he figured. What do you say to the kid you deserted? What could he say to her that would make it all right?

"I'll help Dad with your stuff," was all he could say around the lump in his throat.

She had gone inside and stood in the living room for a long time looking at the row of pictures of him that stopped in grade seven. She didn't say anything. Before too long, she had gone to bed in the room that Holden had made up for her. He had put one of his paintings on the wall, but she didn't say anything about it.

It was strange. It was such a strange day. All that he expected her to say and do, she didn't say or do. She had just drifted off to bed.

She didn't even say good night.

Holden had gone right back up to the attic and drank himself to sleep. He didn't even want to paint. Now that she was back, he couldn't remember what he had been painting for, all that time.

Now, he starts to read again. He takes another slug of whiskey.

"You know," says his mother from the doorway, "you shouldn't drink."

"Yeah? Like you should talk. Besides, you shouldn't spy. This is my room. You aren't invited," Holden says bitterly.

"Holden ... "

"Yes, *Mother*?"

"I don't drink anymore. Maybe you could learn from my mistakes."

"I doubt it."

"Holden?"

"What?"

"Look at me. I'm dying, okay? I'm paying for it."

"All right, Mom, fine."

"Holden ... " she says pleadingly.

"Oh, go away, Mom. Please ... "

She does, turning and walking heavily down the stairs. Wait, he wants to call out. I didn't mean it! But he doesn't; he just sinks back into the couch again and rests the book over his face. Nothing he ever wants to say comes out of his mouth right. He wants to tell her he's sorry. But more than that, he wants her to say that *she's* sorry.

He wants to hear her say it.

He may be a different person now, but he's still the same boy that she left behind. Why won't she acknowledge it? He wants more than anything in the world for her to come over and hug him or muss his hair like she used to, but since she got back she hasn't even touched him. His *mom*.

He can hear them banging furniture around downstairs. When his mom came home, she said she was totally shocked that nothing had changed since she left. That, basically, no one had vacuumed since she took off. She said, "things are going to change around here."

So now they're ripping down pictures and moving stuff around and getting new things. Holden takes another long drink, savoring the burn. Like she's going to be around to enjoy it, anyway – she came home to die, right?

He shakes his head and drops the book on the floor with a thud.

He goes back into the corner and pulls out the painting of Cassie. Another relationship that he destroyed, he figures. He pulls out his brushes and drops a streak of black onto the painting and smears it over her body. He'll paint her some clothes, he thinks. He'll try to fix the damage that he did.

Cassie repeats the series of steps again and again. The dance room is empty. Everyone else is at dinner, or has gone home. Again and again she repeats the motion. She can't seem to get the *tour en l'air* to work: she is landing too heavily. It's traditionally the male dancer's step, anyway, but at an all-girls school, the rules get changed. She's determined to nail it for her audition. In the mirror she looks awkward. She does it again, sweat trickling down her brow. Again.

Someone claps. Cassie jumps, startled.

"Oh, Sina! I didn't hear you come in. Wow! I'm wiped out – this dance is killing me."

"It looks great, though," Sina says sincerely.

"No, it isn't right," Cassie says emphatically. "I have to work on that middle step, it's not working ... sorry, not your problem, I know."

"Hey, we're best friends, right? Your problems are my problems, *ma chérie*."

"I guess," she laughs. "Forget it. Hang on a sec, would you, I'll grab my stuff and we can walk back together."

"Actually ... "

"What?"

"I can't. I'm meeting someone."

"Meeting someone? Who? A mysterious stranger?"

"Sort of. I don't know. I feel weird telling you this. I know you don't like him."

"Who are you meeting, Sina? What's the big deal?"

"Mr. Mitchell," Sina says, after a brief hesitation.

Cassie stares at her friend. "I don't get it. Why?"

"I'm going to help him with a project," Sina answers, lowering her eyes suggestively. "Mr. Mitchell, let me help you with that ... I'm kidding, actually it's a group of us in the Biology Club, we're doing a video thing."

"Sina! You're impossible," Cassie laughs. "Go on, then. You don't want to be late for your date."

She waits for Sina to leave, then takes a deep breath and starts again from the beginning. *Jeté, step, pas de chat, arabesque*, turn and bend, step turn. *Tour en l'air*. She stops. She missed ... again. In her heart, she hears the thundering chords of the music. Again. *Allongé*. She feels her muscles protest, aching and burning. Stretch some more. Again.

"Hey, stranger," Holden says, shifting uncomfortably on Matt's front porch. The cat rubs up against his leg, and he fights the urge to kick it.

"Hey! Long time no see."

"Yeah. I just thought ... you know, if you're not busy, that we could hang out."

"You have to ask?" Matt says, looking at his friend's bloodshot eyes and straggly hair. "You look like shit, by the way. What better thing would I rather do?"

"It's been a while, I thought you and Taylor ... " Holden shrugs.

"No way, man. That's over. Way over."

"Really? What happened?"

"I don't know. She's got her training and stuff and she just never had time to ... well ... whatever. She's busy, okay? I'm busy. We're just too busy to ... ah, forget it."

"Had a fight, did you?"

"Yeah," he sighs. "I guess. Another one. Man. I just don't get it."

"Girls, huh," says Holden, with sympathy.

"You know what? I'm hungry. Let's go get some grub."

Holden follows Matt to the car. "So, what happened?" he asks, settling into the seat.

"I don't know. Really, actually, I don't. Things were great. Then after New Year's, she just didn't seem to want to have much to do with me, and I've been having major hockey practices and stuff and I didn't have that much time to really notice. Then," he shrugs, "then, it just sort of tapered off."

"Really? You're going to let that happen?"

"You're one to talk, Mr. I'm-in-love-with-Cassie."

"That's different."

"Different how?"

"Well, for one thing, she doesn't know. And for another, we didn't ... you know."

"Huh. I guess. It's not like we ... I mean, we only did it once." Matt glowers at the steering wheel. It was after they did *it* that Taylor started acting, well, withdrawn. Then she wouldn't let him touch her – she didn't even really seem to want to kiss him. He shudders. Maybe it was him. Maybe she was grossed out by his disgusting body.

"Hey, Holden," he says. "D'you think I'm fat?"

"You're asking me that? What are you, a girl?"

"I'm serious. Who else can I ask?"

"Okay, okay. Let me think. Okay. You're not fat, all right? You're big. That's all. Maybe you should work out more. Get more buff." He shrugs. "What do I know? Look at me."

"Maybe you're right," Matt says, turning the car sharply to the left.

"Hey, what're you doing?"

"I just decided that maybe I'm not hungry after all. Crank the tunes, would you? We'll go cruising, baby."

"Sure." This is great, Holden thinks, leaning back. This is the way it should be, two guys hanging out together. No parents. No girls. Perfect.

January. It's a new year. He even went to his first AA meeting. Okay, well, he didn't stay long. It was pretty morbid, all those people sitting around on folding chairs in a big dusty church. It was everything he imagined, only worse. *Hello, my name is Holden, and I'm an alcoholic*. Well, he couldn't say it. He couldn't stay. All that higher power crap, forget it. He doesn't need that. Besides, he's been sober for two weeks. That's a long time, for Holden.

He doesn't need to drink. He can do it himself.

He takes a long drag of the joint that he had in his pocket. Who needs liquor, anyway? Pot is just as good, and the hangover is nothing compared to drinking. He listens to Matt talking about Taylor and feels pretty relaxed and pretty good. He even forgets about his mom for a while. He forgets about everything except sitting there with Matt.

"You're a good buddy," he tells his friend.

"Yeah," Matt agrees. "That's for sure."

Mark Mitchell cried when he saw the news. The bodies of the whales washed up on shore. He was paralyzed. What could he do? He wanted to go, but what would he do there? It was unbelievable. This kind of thing just didn't happen in Canada – it didn't. It was illegal. Wasn't it?

He himself had been on boats observing that very pod of whales. Somewhere, he had pictures of them, alive and moving through the cold northern water where they would never swim again. It was a resident pod, a family. *His* family inasmuch as he had studied and loved those whales, knew about their relationships and respected their boundaries.

His wife held him and rocked him like a child while the baby slept in the cradle.

"I can't believe it," he said. "I can't believe it."

In total, five whales were killed and the rest of the pod had just disappeared. Where did they go?

So now, he stands at the front of his classroom and looks at the sleepy, uninterested students. Some of them stare out the window. The snow that fell last week has started to melt and turn to slush, and as far as the eye can see, the world looks grey and dirty and hopeless. There are puddles of water on the floor from snow melting from shoes. He sighs.

"Okay," he says. "We're going to talk about the whale slaughter."

He tells them what happened and tries to swallow past the lump in his throat. Can't they see? He knows they are thinking about their next dance, their next audition. He knows they don't really care.

"They're going to catch the people who did this," he tells them. "They'll be caught."

A couple of girls watch him sympathetically and nod. A couple of them come up to him after class and tell them they were really moved by what happened. They lean close to him and gaze up at him with their flirtatious eyes.

They don't care, he realizes. They don't even care about this.

But he's going to do something. He's going to turn his project into something more meaningful. Something powerful. He's going to get his message across.

TEN

"You know what we should do?"

"What, Mom?" Holden says, trying not to sound irritated.

It's just that she's always in his face. She probably wants them to join family AA or something. He scowls at her, standing there with her hands on her hips, wearing an apron like Betty Crocker. Except she isn't. You can see that from the lines around her eyes. The blotches on her skin. The hollows in her cheeks. She looks wasted.

"What should we do, Mom? I don't have all day to chat."

"I was thinking about the cabin," she says dreamily.

"What cabin?"

"You know, the cabin. We used to go there all the time, when you were ... little."

"Oh. That. We haven't gone there since you ... forget it. Anyway, Dad probably sold it or something. Ask him."

"I think we should go," she says, sounding quite determined.

So it's decided.

Holden glares moodily out the window as the car, stuffed with sleeping bags and food and junk, weaves along the road to the lake. It's freezing. It's February, for God's sake. No one goes to a summer cabin in February. His mom is actually singing in the front seat along with the static on the radio. He stares at the back of her head and wills her to shut up. He can see tiny threads of silver woven into her once dark hair. She isn't that old, he figures, but he guesses she did a lot of living from the time she left until now. He doesn't want to ask her exactly what she did. He figures she'll tell him when she wants to, if she wants to...

"Come on, Holden, sing with us! Up, up and away in my beautiful balloon ... "

"No, thanks."

His dad is singing. This is unbelievably absurd. Everyone has gone crazy. Now that they are out of Victoria and making their way north up the Island, the terrain is changing. Out the window, all he can see is about a million miles of farmers' fields. A few cows braving the cold, chewing on frozen grass. Popsicles. He breathes hard on the window, then traces a cow's face in the steam. His nails are black and blue with paint. Idly, he starts picking at them.

"Watch out," his mom says. "You almost hit those girls."

He looks out and sees two blonde women on bicycles.

"Hey!" he says.

"What is it?"

"Nothing. Just someone I know," he says, slumping back down in the seat.

"On the bicycle?" asks his mom. "The girl?"

Holden looks pointedly out the window. Like there is anyone else within a hundred miles except for the incessant traffic.

"A girlfriend?"

"No. Forget it." He sighs. "Matt's girlfriend. Doesn't matter."

"Is that why Matt isn't around so much anymore?"

"Yeah, I guess," mumbles Holden. "Something like that."

They start singing again. Holden clutches his ears and groans. "For heaven's sake," he says. "Just stop."

The cabin is falling apart. The boards creak and groan as they climb the steps to the front porch. Some of them have rotted and fallen away.

"That was quick," says his mom quietly. "Only five years."

"A lot can happen in five years," snaps Holden.

"I know," she says, sitting down on an old bench facing the lake. "I know."

At least the lake isn't frozen when they awaken the next day. The sun is shining, and if you could get past the cold, you might imagine it was summer after all.

Holding his breath, Holden swings out on the rope suspended from the red-barked arbutus but doesn't let go. He used to love this when he was a kid. He swings back and forth over the lake and looks down into the shallows. He can't see anything in the murky water. He used to do this all the time, he reminds himself. He wasn't afraid until he was eight. He looks up at his mom sitting on the porch. She isn't watching him. He is shaking, would do anything for a drink. Maybe this is the best cure, he thinks, winding up again on the swing. Or maybe he'll drown. That would be ironic, he thinks, letting go.

"Yaaahooooooo!"

The icy water rushes over his head. It's been years since he went swimming. He chokes and sputters, then takes a few experimental strokes. That's better, he thinks, his body adjusting slowly. He quickly swims to the raft in an amateur crawl/dog-paddle. The air seems colder than the water. He hoists himself up the old ladder and tries to sit on the wood. It's freezing. He could use a drink, but he'll have to swim back to get it. The water wasn't cold enough to shock the need from his body. Shit. He drops back into the water again. It's clouded over since he woke up; big round drops of rain are plopping into the lake. He floats on his back so he doesn't have to look down into the lake reeds.

When they used to come up here, he'd always been allowed to invite a friend. Of course, he always brought Matt. Never Cassie. Because Cassie was a girl. It just wouldn't have been right. The wind blows across the surface and makes him shiver. Gooseflesh rises on his arms.

It used to be so hot in the summer, Holden muses. He remembers it being so hot every night, so hot they had to sleep with fans and the windows open. Now, it is not hot.

They have never been here in winter before; it seems like it should be warmer, that some kind of colossal mistake has been made by the weather. If he squints, he can see his mom is on the deck of the cabin, watching him now. It's still so strange to have her back. Her and her seven million bottles of drugs that fill the fridge. Not illegal drugs, but drugs that keep her from getting sicker, that keep her alive. His eyes sting. What a fucked-up family, he thinks. What a bunch of losers.

He tries to remember what it was like before.

Holden and Matt jostle each other in the back seat.

"Mom, Matt's bugging me!"

"Holden ... "

"What?"

"Just settle down back there, guys," his father interrupts. "We'll be there any minute."

Matt sticks out his tongue and crosses his eyes.

Holden shifts across the seat and pinches his friend's leg.

"Mrs. Stenopolis! Mrs. Stenopolis! Holden's pinching me!"

"Holden ... just stop." His mother's hands are shaking as she lights another cigarette.

"You shouldn't smoke in the car," Holden says smugly." You're filling our young lungs up with black gunk. You're killing us."

The boys immediately start coughing and gasping.

"Boys! Settle down!"

Those were the good times, Holden thinks, reflecting back on it. They'd go to the lake and he and Matt would stay in the water all day, every day, swimming and diving and goofing around. They built forts and rafts and all kinds of stuff. Then his mom started acting weird, staring off into space all the time.

Then she went away.

Thinking back on it, Holden reflects, the best part was the water. Swimming across to the island in the middle. Him and Matt. Things are sure different now.

He swims towards the shore, his muscles protesting

in the cold. This must have been how cold it was when that girl fell in the whale pond, he thinks suddenly. February. Then he pushes the thought out of his mind.

"Aren't you cold?" his mom calls. "You should take a hot shower and get something warm on."

Yeah, right, he thinks to himself, without saying anything. Where were you the last five years? Maybe I've been cold the whole time. Did you ever think about that?

Cassie's awake again. Through her half-closed eyes, Sina watches her friend crying in her pillow, shoulders shaking.

"Hey," she whispers.

"What?"

"Are you okay?"

Cassie sniffs. "Bad dream, I guess. You don't have any more of those pills, do you?"

Sina shakes her head. "Sorry."

"It's okay."

They lie in silence for a while, listening to the rain fall on the roof and into the eaves. Sina tries to stay awake, but she can't. Pretty soon, Cassie can hear her gently snoring.

She rolls over. The clock says 2:04. Too early to get up, that's for sure. She closes her eyes again. Not water, she thinks. Dream about dancing. Dream about Holden. Anything.

Her eyes drift shut.

"How does that make you feel?" Cassie's father is asking.

Cassie crouches in the closet, holding her breath. She's just little – eight years old. What is she doing here? She knows that she has been told never to play in her father's office while he is working.

The patient starts to cry.

Why is her father making this lady cry?

"It's okay to cry, but you have to talk about why this makes you feel so sad."

Cassie sniffs in the closet. How does that make you feel? Her father is always asking her that question, too. Usually she says, "Good!" or "Happy!" or even "Mad!" But she never says more. This lady is talking and talking. Cassie closes her eyes. Talking and talking.

" ... dreaming about killer whales ... I know it's ridiculous ... "

Cassie jumps to attention. Killer whales? She presses her eye against the tiny hole in the door. She can see the back of the lady's head. The bright red mop of hair. She can see her father, staring out the window. Somehow, because she is dreaming, she can see what he is thinking. He is imagining her mom, holding a baby. Her brother? He is thinking about that.

The lady is still talking, then stops abruptly.

"But how does that make you feel?" her father asks.

"Cassie?"

But that's me, she wants to say. That's me.

"Cassie!"

"What, Daddy?"

"What are you doing in here? I've told you a hundred times, young lady. That is enough. Now, I have to punish you. How does that make you feel?"

In spite of herself, Cassie giggles. How does that make you feel?

His hand against her cheek is so startling that she forgets to cry, just sits down on the carpet with a dull thud. Slowly, in the freckles, the outline of his hand appears.

"Daddy?"

Cassie jerks awake. 3:15. Not bad. A whole hour. And she didn't dream about the water. She yawns and stretches. Maybe it will be okay, then. Maybe she'll be able to get back to sleep.

"So, have you guys made up yet?"

"Hey, Holden. Where have you been?"

"We went to the cabin. Don't ask. So, have you called her yet, or what?"

"Not exactly."

"No? You're an idiot. Are you going to?"

He shrugs. "I don't know. Maybe it's too late."

"Asshole."

"Are you going to call Cassie?"

"Nope," says Holden, pretending not to flinch at the sound of her name. Cassie. He sighs. "Actually, I have a date tonight."

"You do?" says Matt, not bothering to disguise his surprise.

"Yup," says Holden, trying to sound cool.

"*You*? Holden?"

"That's me."

"With *who*?"

"Jasmine."

"Jasmine? Jasmine-from-English-class Jasmine?"

"The one and only," answers Holden smugly.

"Wow. I didn't know you even knew her."

"Yeah. She's in my art class. We hang out sometimes."

"So you have a date ... stud."

"Jealous?" smirks Holden.

"Nope."

"Liar!"

"Jasmine," repeats Matt, baffled. "Who would of thought?"

Holden's dad is waiting for him when he gets home.

"Son, we have to talk," he says in his serious voice.

"Not now, Dad, I have a date. I gotta go."

"Holden, it's your mother."

"Oh yeah? What is it this time? She renovating my room?"

"Not this time, son," he says. Something in his tone makes Holden's blood run cold.

"What's wrong?"

"She took a turn for the worse, Holden. The doctors think it might be pneumonia. She's in the hospital. It would be nice if you went to see her."

"Yeah?" says Holden, pretending not to care. "Maybe tomorrow. I told you, I got a date tonight."

He pushes past his father up the stairs and tries to hide the fact that his knees are shaking.

A couple of swigs of Wild Turkey later, he calms down. He needs it. He has a date. He hasn't been on a date for a long time, in spite of the fact that Matt tells him that a bunch of girls have a crush on him. Well, he's not good enough for Cassie. She didn't send any response to the Valentine he mailed her. So forget it. He'll go out with someone else. He doesn't need the stress of waiting around for her.

Besides, he can't deal with it all. There's his mom. She's there, then she's gone for, like, his whole life, then she's back and it's starting to be almost normal, and now she's going to get sick and die. He blinks back his tears.

He looks around and catches sight of the Cassie painting, sitting crooked on the floor. That just makes him feel worse.

"Damn you, Cassie," he says. "It's your fault."

He walks over to it and stomps heavily in the middle, his foot tearing through the canvas. He thinks about Jasmine, his date for tonight. She's cute and talented and interesting. Her sculptures just blow him away – giant clay abstracts. But she's not Cassie, she'll never be Cassie. He takes another long swallow and lifts his foot off the painting.

Cassie doesn't want anything to do with him. How long will it take him to get that through his thick head?

He looks at the clock. Seven-thirty. He said he'd meet her at seven. He's late. Not a cool way to make an impression. Without bothering to change, he jogs out the door into the freezing evening air. Drizzle flattens his hair and soaks through his jacket.

She's still waiting when he gets there, at a table with three of her friends. As soon as they see him come in, they start giggling, and he feels like a loser. What are they laughing at? How old are they, anyway?

"Sorry I'm late," he says to Jasmine, ignoring the others. "Missed the bus, I guess."

"That's okay," she says. "That's cool. You ready to go?"

"Sure."

They make their way down the slippery sidewalk to the exhibition. Once, her foot skates out from underneath her, and she almost falls to the ground. He reaches out to grab her arm and ends up keeping his hand there.

"For safety reasons," he tells her gravely. He can feel the warmth of her body under her clothes.

She laughs, flashing her even white teeth. In the street light, her nose ring looks sparkly and dangerous. He starts to relax. She's so pretty, it's hard not to like her. "What do you think of this one?" She stops in front of a huge canvas, smeared with beige blobs of paint.

"Um," says Holden. "What do you think?"

"I think it's great, it's fantastic. You should do stuff like this."

Really? he thinks, staring at the picture which looks like bird crap.

"What is it?" he asks someone else. "What is it a picture of?"

The woman points to the tag in the corner.

"Ah," he says. "Beige Number Seven. Obviously."

He glances at his watch. Nine o'clock. In the far corner, a group of paintings catches his eye. He wanders over, leaving Jasmine admiring Beiges Number Four through Fourteen. Not his kind of art, that's for sure. But the paintings in the corner – what is it about them?

Maybe it is the red hair of the model, posing on the pink chair. He looks at them thoughtfully. The artist has done an excellent job of arranging the colors so they are not jarring, but so they each bring out the other. He's also done something interesting with the light – the shadows are not quite right, but lend the painting some mystery, some sense of disproportion. Other than the shadows, the painting is as exact as a photograph. He walks to the side and looks at them from an angle. He frowns thoughtfully. What is it, something to do with the medium? He himself doesn't use acrylics that much, preferring the heavy layering quality of oil. But these ...

"Yikes," says Jasmine behind him, passing him another Dixie cup of wine. "Looks like Anne of Green Gables gone bad."

"You don't like it?"

"No, thanks," she shudders, leaning against him. "It's awful."

He can smell her hair. It smells like green apples. For a second, he closes his eyes, inhaling the scent. Then he pushes her away. "I like it. I think it's the best thing here."

"Really? You're kidding me," she says, laughing.

"No, I really like it," he says vehemently.

Holden drinks the wine in one swallow. "And," he adds, clearing his throat, "I think Beige Number Whatever is horrible."

She stares at him, squinting, not unlike his mom. As if maybe something disgusting is hanging from his nose. "Holden, are you drunk?"

"Oh for God's sake," he says, pushing by her towards the door.

He stumbles. Great. Makes him look drunk when he's not. He's not.

How could he have thought she was so cute? She's an idiot.

He walks home. All the way. It's freezing cold, and he walks for miles with no coat, ignoring the fact that his nails are turning blue. Clouds block out the stars and moon; he is left with the lights of passing cars and the street lamps.

As he turns on to his street, the light above him pops and burns out with a loud fizzle.

Somehow, this makes him feel better.

He's never been able to talk to any girl other than Cassie. Maybe there is only one girl in the world for him and he's already blown it with her. Maybe he has nothing else to look forward to now for the rest of his life.

ELEVEN

"Cassie, you have to come with me," Sina is saying. "Please? I asked Mrs. Bracken, and she said you could. Come on. Please? I need the moral support."

"Of course, I'll come with you, silly," Cassie says, trying to focus her attention on her friend. "I'm sorry. I'm just distracted. Tell me about it again."

Sina tells her: She has been asked to audition for a part on a soap opera. She'll be reading for the part of the daughter of two doctors on the show, who have spent the last million years divorcing each other, marrying other cast members, then getting back together. The daughter has been in a mental institute for ten years, but has been released into her parents' custody.

"Sounds like real life," Cassie teases her friend.

"Still," Sina says seriously, "I never thought I'd be on a soap, you know? But it's a start! And it's filmed here. What more could I want?"

"What did your mom say?"

"I'm not going to tell her, in case I don't get it. It'd be like a jinx, right?"

"Slow down!" Cassie laughs, as Sina trips over her words.

"I know! I'm just totally psyched! I have to find something to wear. Oh my God! I can't believe this!" She does a quick dance in the middle of the room, flinging a handful of clean laundry at Cassie.

"It's great," says Cassie, pulling a sock out of her hair. "Really great. I'm happy for you."

"Call her, man, I can't stand it," Holden says, glaring at Matt.

"I don't know."

"Just *call* her. You're driving me crazy. You fight with Taylor too much. You're nuts. You're wrecking a good thing. What was it this time?"

"She ... I don't know. I wanted her to come diving with me, so I signed her up again. It was stupid. She doesn't want to do it. I'm an idiot," Matt says, leaning back on the moth-eaten couch in Holden's attic room.

"That's true," Holden agrees.

Matt hesitates and picks up the phone. Holden watches from across the room, where he is dabbing at a painting. He pretends he isn't listening, but he is. I'm one to talk, he thinks. He won't phone Cassie. But what would he say? Sorry for picturing you naked? Sorry for liking you? Sorry for writing?

Matt turns his back. Holden can hear him apologizing.

"I'm sorry, I'm an insensitive jerk. I really am sorry. I won't ask you again, I promise ... "

Then, "Really? Great! I'll be right there. I'd love to come. Great."

Holden winces. Why is it so easy for Matt? He should just call Cassie and explain about the painting and tell her how he feels and then let her be angry. Jesus.

Matt's laughing, so *he* must be okay. Holden gives him the thumbs up and turns back to his painting. He wants to get the light right. Light is the key; he saw that at the exhibit when he went. He has started again with some sketches of Cassie, and he is dabbing paint on much more nervously than usual. The colors are so delicate, and it's important that they be perfect.

Finally, he hears Matt clearing his throat.

"Oh, sorry," he says. "Forgot you were here. How did that go?"

"You were listening to every word, you asshole. You know what she said."

"Listening? Me?" Holden feigns innocence. "I would never ... "

"Jerk. Anyway, she forgives me. Again. So I guess I'm an idiot, but I still get the girl! I'm outta here."

"See ya," says Holden, turning back to the painting.

He sips whiskey from a coffee mug. He has his own stash up in the attic. Perfect. He managed to get into the liquor store without being asked for ID and his dad is being more generous with money lately, probably distracted by all his mom's ups and downs. On her good days, it seems like she might be okay, but on her bad days ... well, he doesn't want to think about those. He takes another healthy swallow. He can't quit yet. There's just too much tension in the house. He bends over the painting and the brush moves loosely in his hand.

Hours later, he's on his knees. The bathroom tile flows and ebbs around Holden's face.

"Oh, God," he moans. "Oh, no."

His stomach retches and heaves, but he can't seem to lift his head up to the toilet.

He hoists himself into the bathtub instead. That's better. His head drops to the side. He presses his cheek against the cool enamel and commands his head to stop spinning.

"Holden!"

"I'm in the bathroom, Dad," Holden mumbles.

"Holden!" his dad shouts again.

"Dad ... I'm in the *bathroom*," Holden calls back with superhuman effort.

The door bursts open.

"Holden, I ... What's wrong with you?"

"Sick ... " he moans.

"Sick how? What's the matter? Holden?" his dad says, worried.

"S'hangover," Holden confesses.

"Oh," his father says with disgust. "That's a different story, then, isn't it."

Before he leaves the room, he turns the shower on full blast.

Holden tries to scream, then finds it's too much trouble. Instead, he just lies there and lets the cold water pound on his face.

This feels right, he thinks. This feels like torture.

I'll go back to AA, he promises himself. This time, I'll really try. I will.

TWELVE

Cassie leans up against a tree. The sap smells tangy and fresh, and sticks to her hair and clothing. She doesn't care. The pink-orange sun is just rising, and it is cool but not freezing. Somewhere, she can hear the song of a bird. Spring is finally coming, and with spring comes summer and with summer comes her big audition. Her one big chance. She leans back against the rough bark and looks into the widening swathe of color. One chance. Cigarette butts litter the ground, and she kicks them angrily out of her sight. No more smoking, not for her. That's over. She doesn't even come out here with Sina anymore; she doesn't want any smoke polluting her lungs.

She thinks Sina understands, hopes she can see that

dancing is more important to Cassie than anything else ever could be.

She shivers under her cotton sweats. She couldn't sleep last night at all, whales leaping into her dreams again and again. She calculates how many times she has had this dream. Nine years since it happened, and then some. That's at least ... three thousand times. Is that possible? She can hardly remember what it is like to sleep without nightmares. She must have some dreamless sleep, she reasons. Or else she'd be dead by now. She points her toes out in front of her, stretching over them. She feels the muscles in her spine stretch out. Three thousand times. She bends over her knees. Lifts her arms behind her. *Allongé*. She stretches.

"Cassie?" A voice interrupts her thoughts and startles her.

"What? Who's that?" She practically jumps out of her skin, the tree scratching her back as she leaps to her feet.

"It's me. Mark, I mean, Mr. Mitchell."

She looks around the tree and sees him standing uncomfortably in the dewy grass.

"What are you doing?" she asks, her voice querulous. "Why are you following me?"

"Cassie, I'm not. I know you think I am, but I'm not. Look, can I talk to you?"

"I guess. But not here." She turns her back on the rising sun. "Not here. I'll meet you in the library. We can talk in the library."

Her hands tremble. What does he want? For a second, she imagines he is going to proposition her. Maybe she should go back to the room and wake Sina up, let her sneak into the stacks and spy in case something happens. In case she needs help. She breathes in sharply. Don't be ridiculous, she tells herself. He's a teacher.

"Morning, Cassidy," the cook calls as she passes her in the hall. "Beautiful morning!"

"Yes, it is," she replies. "I'm just going to the library to meet Mr. Mitchell."

"Okay, dear. Have a nice day!"

She doesn't know why, but it seems important to tell someone where she is going.

"Cassie?"

He's sitting at one of the tables, in a red chair. She sees the librarian in the office, drinking from a china cup. Good. Nothing can happen, then. Mr. Mitchell looks embarrassed. The chair squeaks as he shifts his weight.

"Oh, hi, Mr. Mitchell," she says, as casually as possible.

"I know you must think this is a little strange," he gestures. "I guess it is. I ... "

She looks at him expectantly. What is he talking about?

"It's just ... I wanted to talk to you about the Seaquarium."

"The Seaquarium?" she repeats numbly. A peculiar metallic taste fills her mouth.

"I wasn't there. I mean, that day, but ... I know you were. Don't get angry ... Cassie. Listen. I think you are in a unique position to take a stand on this ... I think it would help. Just listen for a minute, please? I know it was you. I saw a bunch of kids, and I remember ... your hair. And I've watched the news reports a hundred times. I ... you look the same. Sorry. I don't want to sound patronizing. But I thought I recognized you, then I checked your records, and I knew it had to be you. So I asked your mom, and she said it was, but that I shouldn't talk about it."

"Oh."

"So something has happened, something awful, and I'm doing a video about the capture of whales. I just want you to watch it. Maybe you can talk a bit on the tape, if you want, about what happened to you, or what you saw ... "

"I can't listen to this. I have to go," Cassie says, barely keeping the panic out of her voice. Her heart beats wildly in her throat. She looks around frantically, her empty stomach churning. "Mr. Mitchell, I know you want to talk about it, but I can't. I just can't."

"Cassie! Before you go ... " He hesitates. He wants to show her the tape he has, but he doesn't want to upset her any more than he already has. He sighs and puts the tape on the table, the black plastic rectangle declaring nothing of the sadness it contains.

She pauses for a minute, her skin pale against her bright hair, her eyes red from sleeplessness. Her eyelid twitches as she stares at the tape.

"What is it?" she says wearily.

"Just watch this. Cassie? Please?"

"All right," she reluctantly agrees. She sits down heavily and resigns herself to watching. Maybe if she does this, he'll leave her alone. He talks while she watches, but she doesn't hear him. She sees the bloody dead bodies of whales on the shore of a northern island. The water is grey and looks impossibly cold, and the land she can glimpse in the background looks barren. The large carcasses are lined up on the beach, almost in a perfect row, like dancers at the barre. The tape wobbles and then cuts to a baby swimming around in an aqua-colored tank. It looks small and desperate as it moves towards the camera and then away. She leans closer to watch. The baby swims upside down in circles around the enclosure, then rolls over and takes a breath. It seems to be swimming in slow motion, and its eyes are curiously flat.

"It's a baby," she says.

"Yes," he answers. "A couple of months old. The baby was caught," he adds, "at the expense of the others."

"What happened to its mother?"

"On the beach," he gestures.

"Oh," she breathes sadly. "Oh my god."

They watch the end of the video in silence. The

baby stops swimming. The tape gets staticky and wiggles and then the camera straightens again. Some men get into the tank and try to force tubes into its throat – for feeding, Mark explains. Cassie shudders.

"That's cruel," she says softly.

The whale flops around and then stills and seems to resign itself to its handlers. The tape flickers and goes black. It clicks loudly when it runs out and begins rewinding loudly.

"Wow," says Cassie. "That was so ... violent."

"Cassie, that baby died. She died. She sort of killed herself – just held her breath and sank. They killed her mother and several members of her family and then she died. We have to stop it. It isn't right. You know that. If you could just ... "

"What? What could I do?" She feels almost angry. What is he asking of her? What can *she* do?

"Cassie," he says, "that baby hadn't even been named yet. It's just one of the many captured whales that dies and is recorded as 'No name' on the records. The video we are putting together is going to be shown on public TV, it will ... well." He stops and looks at her seriously. She seems a million miles away. "Just think about it. Please?"

"I'll think about it. Fine. Okay."

Jerk, she thinks, dashing down the hall. Asshole. Her fists are clenched by her sides, bitten nails digging into her palms. Her anger keeps the tears from flowing until she makes it into the privacy of the dance studio.

It's seven o'clock in the morning. What is he doing there anyway? Why does he have to be one of those teachers that are always around? At least he doesn't live there, like the matrons. On the other hand, it seems at this school there are always teachers around at all hours of the day, running clubs and rehearsals and doing extra things.

Cassie cries and cries, until she is dry. She sits on the wood floor in a patch of sun and glowers out the window. She thinks about the baby whale. God damn him, she thinks. Now she has to do something.

She sits on the floor for a long time, running her fingers up and down the seams between the boards. Sometimes she looks up at the door, relieved to see he isn't there, looking at her and waiting for her to do something.

Like she could have done something then. Like she could have reached into the pool and pulled the girl out.

She squints into the mirror, trying to see the little girl she once was. She can't see anything but her teenaged self staring back. She pulls her hair back into a knot and begins to practice her audition dance. *Ronds de jambe* and *allongés*. She stretches until it burns and tears sting her eyes. Nothing helps her, she thinks furiously. Only dancing. It's her only escape.

The canvas has never looked so white, Holden thinks angrily, swiping the black brush across the middle. It only accentuates the rest of the glaring emptiness. More black. More, then more. His mom went out and bought him some new canvases and stuff, after she got out of the hospital. She's not doing very well, though; even an idiot would be able to see that much. She weighs about as much as a blade of grass. And when she breathes, it's so loud her curtains quiver. She was sleeping this morning, and he went in and looked at her and touched her face. Her skin felt as thin and insubstantial as crepe paper.

Anyway, she bought him this stuff, and then his dad came upstairs and said, "It would be nice if you painted your mother a picture, and not one of *those ridiculous whale things* either." The words *if you ever want money for brushes again* were mentioned. His dad obviously doesn't understand, he thinks spitefully. He has nothing to paint except the whales. Nothing. That's all that lives inside him, just killer whales. And Cassie, but that's different. She lives in a place inside him that's closer to his heart. What else?

He could paint her up a big bottle of Wild Turkey. She'd probably like that. God knows, she used to. He remembers coming home from school and finding her sitting in the living room in front of the TV, clutching her coffee mug full of booze, staring out the window, dressed to the nines. Once she asked him to paint some bars across the window. He didn't understand. Bars? He was only a kid. "Forget it," she'd said then. "You wouldn't understand." And she was right. He didn't. He doesn't now.

His head is throbbing. Tylenol only does so much for a hangover. He's had about a million glasses of water and that hasn't helped much either.

"Shit," he swears.

He looks around the empty loft, and thinks about Cassie dancing. She was truly amazing to watch. Her arms reached up forever; her body snapped and whirled like elastic, almost like she *became* the dance. He wonders if she knows how talented she is. His paintbrush twirls idly through the red and orange. Before he can stop himself, he's painting her again. His brush sometimes has a mind of its own.

Sometimes he can separate himself from it, just a little, and can watch the painting create itself.

In the background waves appear. Blue-grey and turbulent. He paints a blue sky, streaked through with white clouds and wind. The air carries autumn leaves, drifting across the front of the picture like a veil. Yes, he thinks. Perfect. The rocky surface is next, giving way to round pebbles and sand. Beach glass, broken and reflecting green and blue. Then driftwood. The wood is the most challenging. He squints at the canvas in the dimming light. He is used to working only in the hazy green-glass world of underwater, so these colors are new to his brush. Sand colors. Brown and grey and white and black. The wood faded and beaten by a million waves. The painting spills out onto the canvas. He turns on the desk lamp, not stopping as dusk falls, not stopping for dinner, or even a drink.

The next time he looks out the window, it's dark again. The stars are out, and the moon is full, shining in the window like a spotlight. He tilts the canvas a little so the moonlight can spill across it. He's almost at the best part.

This time he paints her with clothes. She appears in the distance, walking along the shore with Max. Her hair is just visible beneath a pale grey hat.

It's the best he's ever done. He can tell right away, by the light of the rising sun when he's finished. He's worked through the night. And the amazing part of that? He hasn't touched a drop. And under the board in the corner there's a full bottle of vodka left in his stash.

So it's done. He sits in the early dawn and stares out the window.

It's done.

School will be starting soon, he thinks, but he doesn't move. Eventually, he goes to his closet and pulls out his jacket. In the pocket is the card of the man who was sitting next to him at the AA meeting. He had grabbed Holden's arm as he tried to sneak out and passed it to him. The guy was familiar, somehow, and Holden had nodded and pocketed the card.

He picks up the phone and dials, his hands shaking.

"This time, it's for real," he says out loud, listening to the phone ringing in the stranger's home.

The man answers, and Holden starts to talk.

THIRTEEN

The school bus is half-empty. Cassie and Sina sit next to each other, each lost in their own private world. Someone rolls an apple down the center aisle. There is jostling and shouting. Outside, rain pours down in sheets. The window is streaked with water.

"Okay," Sina says. "I'm only going to go through this one more time. Okay?"

"Sure," Cassie says, dragging herself back to the moment. "Tell me again."

"Okay. So I read the part, right? Then the director, this guy John, says, 'Read it one more time, please,' so I did. Then they asked me to go sit in the waiting room, right? And so I do, and I'm sitting there and sitting there and a bunch of other people come and go, and I'm the only one still there. And then I go back in, and he says, 'One more time, please Sina,' so I do it, right? Then he says, 'We'll be in touch with your agent.' So? What do you think?"

"I think you did great, Sina, and he'll be in touch with your agent. You have to stop thinking about it – you'll drive yourself crazy."

"I know, it's just it's been a month already. It's been so long. You know?"

Cassie looks out at the grey spring day. It rains in Vancouver all the time. It's incessant. But she doesn't remember it ever raining *this* much before. Traffic passes by, splashing pedestrians with puddle spray. She presses her face against the cool glass.

"You'll get the part," she says. "I know you will."

For some reason, she doesn't feel as happy for Sina as she should. What she feels is closer to sad. Or jealous. Maybe both. She thinks about her own upcoming audition, then puts it out of her head altogether. She won't get it; she shouldn't even think about it. Just in case, she has set up some other auditions for local dance companies. They probably won't take her either. She sighs. Her mood feels as damp and dark and melancholy as the pavement outside.

"Where are we going, anyway?"

Sina shrugs. "I don't know. Mr. Mitchell said it was a surprise."

"Whatever. I could do without Mr. Mitchell's surprises," Cassie says grouchily.

"Why don't you like him?"

"Oh, I don't know. It's a long story. Maybe I'll tell you one day," she says, looking sideways at her friend. "It's not a big deal, don't look so worried. I just think he should butt out of other people's business, that's all."

"Well, I, for one, think he's pretty cute."

"You and every other girl in the school," agrees Cassie. "He is cute, okay? He's just ... weird. I just don't like him. This sucks. We better be back in time for rehearsal."

The bus turns on Georgia Street, heading towards Stanley Park. The traffic is heavy. As usual, only two lanes are open. Rain rolls off all the cars, making them look alive in the dim light. Why is it always raining when they have to go on field trips? she wonders. Every memory she has of any field trip in her entire school career has featured rain. Except that day they went to the Seaquarium. She frowns. It wasn't raining then. It was cold and clear. She can remember looking up at the clear blue sky, thinking it looked warmer than it was. It was awfully cold. Especially after the whales splashed them and they were wet and huddled together for warmth downstairs. She remembers playing tag with Matt and Holden in the tunnels, and hide-and-go-seek. They were being silly and giggling about the octopus, she remembers that, too. And then ...

They were hiding in the corner when it happened. She shudders.

"Cassie, are you okay?"

"Sure, I was just ... it's nothing. Someone must have walked on my grave, I guess," she shrugs.

The bus winds its way deeper into the park.

"Yuck," says Sina. "This rain is awful."

The tires screech as the bus turns a sharp corner, pulling to a stop in front of the Vancouver Aquarium.

"You've got to be kidding," Cassie says out loud.

"Hey," says Sina, "I haven't been here since I was a little kid. This is great!"

"Sina."

"What?"

"I'm not going in. Forget it. Mr. Damn Mitchell can just go to hell."

"Cassie, what's wrong?"

Cassie scowls and looks out the window. "Didn't I tell you," she hisses, "I'm against keeping whales in captivity. I won't pay money to go in there. I won't go in there. Okay? I won't."

She closes her eyes and sees the images from the tape he showed her splashed across the back of her eyelids. How could he? she thinks. What is he trying to do?

"Oh. Okay. I'm surprised that Mr. Mitchell would bring us ... "

"Everyone off," Mr. Mitchell calls, rubbing his hands

together. "We're here. Look lively, everyone."

On her way past, Cassie shoots him a glare. "I'm not going in," she says witheringly, "and you can't make me. So forget it, Mr. Mitchell. Forget it."

"Sorry, Mr. Mitchell," whispers Sina. "I guess I can't go in either."

"But ... "

"Forget it!" Cassie calls over her shoulder as she runs into the rain. "Just forget it!"

The girls run through the rain that sinks through their clothes to their skin. The fabric clings and sticks uncomfortably. Within a few minutes, they get to the main road and climb on to the city bus heading downtown. Between them, they have forty-three dollars. The stolen day stretches ahead of them, damp and dreary.

"I have to be back at school in time for practice," Cassie reminds her friend. "We can do anything, as long as we're back before five."

They go to the mall, of course, where it's dry. But trying on clothes gets boring pretty quickly when they don't have enough money to buy anything. Besides, they stand out in the crowd in their school uniforms, the dark kilts and blue ties and blazers. Cassie half-expects the truant police to swoop down on them and carry them back to the Aquarium. She frowns.

"I thought Mr. Mitchell was all opposed to aquariums."

"He is," Sina says.

"How do you know?"

"Oh, didn't I tell you? That project I was working on with him? It's a video about whales in captivity and stuff. I don't know. Maybe they're doing something right at this one? Or maybe he was going to burst in and start telling them to release the whales. Who knows?"

"You're working on that, too?"

"Are *you*?"

"I'm thinking about it, I guess. I don't want to talk about it."

The girls make their way down Granville Street towards the bus stop, past shoe stores and pawn shops and porn palaces.

"Not much of a day, huh," says Sina. "Considering how much trouble we're going to get into, it feels like we should have done something really bad."

"Like what?"

"I don't know. We should be getting drunk or something."

Cassie sighs. "I have rehearsal. I can't."

"We should still do something, though."

"Like what?"

"Hey," says Sina, "I know! We could get a tattoo."

"No way. No thanks. Not me."

"Honestly, Cassie, you're such a wuss."

They keep walking. The wet sidewalk smells like urine and cigarettes and pollution. Street people beg them for change. Cassie's skin crawls. She feels like she needs to get home and take a shower. Her uniform skirt sticks uncomfortably to her legs.

"Uck," says Sina. "Let's get out of here."

"Wait! How about that?"

Cassie is pointing to a sign outside a tiny shop that looks like a salon: "Belly button piercing done here!"

It's the sound of the piercing gun snapping that makes Cassie faint. When she comes to, Sina is dribbling cold water on her face.

"They said I should dump the whole glass on you," she whispers conspiratorially, "but that seemed too harsh."

Cassie looks around; the room wobbles uncomfortably.

"What happened?"

"You fainted! Silly. Look at mine!" Sina lifts her shirt, a tiny ring through her navel.

"Cool," says Cassie, looking away.

She can feel her own ring tugging at the skin around her belly button. She has to dig her nails into the palm of her hand to keep from fainting again. The clock on the wall says 3:30.

"We should go," she says, getting carefully off the table. "I don't want to be late."

When Holden gets home from the meeting, he is surprised to see his father at the kitchen table, head in his hands. He's wearing an old plaid shirt that clashes with the red-checkered tablecloth. Some dead flowers fill a vase in front of him.

"Dad?"

"Oh, Holden. I didn't hear you come in."

"What is it, Dad? Has something happened?" His voice catches. "To Mom?"

"She ... " His voice trails off.

"Dad?"

"She ... No. She's in the hospital again. Hospice. She won't be coming home."

It's the first time Holden has ever seen his father cry.

He isn't prepared for what he sees at the hospital. His mother, so small and pale, is made even smaller and paler by the machines around her bed, and those awful green sheets.

"Mom?" he says tentatively.

"Hey, it's you ... " she says, her eyes half open.

"How are you?"

"Not so good," she coughs.

The cough is so deep that Holden can feel it in the soles of his feet. How can she breathe?

"Oh, Mom," he sighs. "I'm sorry this happened to you."

"My fault," she croaks. "Mine. Don't you ever do what I did."

"What did you do?"

She smiles. "What *didn't* I do?"

"Oh."

"Your dad has been really good to me," she whispers hoarsely. "I want you to remember that. I thought when I left that you two would get closer and sort of ... fill the void. God, I was wrong. I was so wrong. I'm sorry. I made ... so many ... mistakes."

"Yeah," Holden says. "I guess you did."

"Anyway ... "

"Yeah," he says. "It's okay."

He takes her hand. The bones are sharp beneath her skin. It's as if that's all there is – parchment-thin skin holding her bones together.

"So I painted something for you," he says, even though she is asleep. "Actually, I painted it for me, but I want you to have it."

He props the painting up on the bedside table. He keeps talking.

"I painted a picture of Cassie, remember her? Anyway, she was around when we were kids. Now she's a ballerina or something. She goes to a boarding school, some arts place, in Vancouver. For the performing arts. So me and Matt bumped into her the other day. Well, actually it was Thanksgiving. On the beach. She was with her dog ... "

Holden talks and talks. He talks for hours. He holds his mom's hand carefully, like it's a baby bird, and he talks.

He talks until the nurse comes in to change the sheets.

"Go home," she says to him. "You can come back tomorrow. It's okay."

So he does. He goes home.

Cassie kicks her old desk drawer angrily.

"I can't believe we got *suspended*," she is saying to Sina on the phone, long distance.

"I know." Sina sniffs. "And you want to know what's worse?"

"What?"

"I didn't get the part."

"Oh, Sina. Oh no. I'm so sorry. That's so ... I thought you would. I'm really sorry."

"I know. Me, too. It just seemed to be the right thing at the right time, you know?"

"Yeah. Do I ever. I'm missing some important rehearsals. Madame was going to help me do some extra work for my audition, and now ... "

"It's just ten days," Sina reminds her.

"I know. It's just ... Being here for ten days feels like a lifetime. And there's nowhere in the house where I can really practice. I just ... I don't know. I guess we were stupid, huh. Or I should say *I* was stupid. It was my stupid idea."

"Don't be such a goof, Cassie. I'm glad I'm not at school right now. I don't want everyone feeling sorry for me because I didn't get the part."

"Oh."

"See, now you feel sorry for me, too."

"Not sorry for you, really. I'm sorry for them for not picking you. You were definitely the prettiest."

"Thanks."

"CASSSSIIIEEE!" Xav yells from the doorway.

"I'm on the phone! Hang on, Sina."

"CAASSSSIIIEEEE?" he calls again.

"What is it, Xav?" she says, with as much patience as she can muster.

"Oh, nothing. Just wondered where you were."

"I'm on the PHONE."

"See?" she says to Sina. "Now I have to put up with my brother, too."

"I have to go, Cassie."

"I know. Me too. Talk to you soon."

Cassie lies back on her child-size bed. Last time she felt like she belonged here she was eight years old. Back then, she loved these ballerina sheets. Now, they're just stupid, but every holiday she sleeps here anyway. Not that she has many holidays. Dancing doesn't take a vacation.

The sheets mock her. Everything is stupid. She has to get out of the house. This house that is so full with her brother and her mom and her dad and his patients.

Car doors slam. Now. She grabs her ballet stuff on her way out. Maybe she can find some place to practice.

The March sun is shining brightly outside, and the bright new colors revive her dark mood. In the front border, daffodils are starting to bloom, and all along the streets, the cherry blossoms are just beginning to form, sprinkling pink frosting over all the bare trees. She walks down the sidewalk, scuffing her feet, past the house, past Matt's house, past the corner store. She stops outside the elementary school and watches the kids in the field, running around the track. Some of them are pushing really hard, running like they are being chased. Others lope around lazily, chatting to the kid in the next lane. The teacher blows her whistle.

Cassie leans on the chain-link fence, watching until the kids are swallowed up by the school. The week extends endlessly before her. The audition looms in only eight short weeks. She shivers, in spite of the sun. A vague suspicion that she just isn't good enough nags at her. Or worse, what if something happens to her between now and then? Maybe she'll fall and twist her ankle, tear a tendon or break a bone. Or maybe she'll hurt her back, or her neck, or her shoulder. She thinks of all the dancing injuries she has had in her life – knees and wrists and ankles and feet. She sighs, kicking a wayward pine cone with her pointed toe. She walks all the way down to the park at the end of the road, the park that stretches for acres just outside of downtown at the end of Dallas Road. Beacon Hill Park, it's called. It's pretty deserted, only ever really busy in the summer months when people are there running and jogging and walking their dogs. Today, she has it almost to herself.

She drops her bag under a tree and looks around to make sure she is truly alone. She flexes her muscles experimentally. The ground is spongier than the wooden floors she is used to, but it will do, right? It's an open space. Finding a bench at just about the right height, she starts going through her barre exercises. She hasn't danced for the last couple of days, and even in that short time her muscles have become creaky and stiff.

She stretches out for a long time, letting the tepid sun warm her back. Again, she whispers. Again. She forces herself to go through the drill one more time. Across the clearing, she can see on old man with a Scottie dog on a lead watching her. Ignore him, she instructs herself. Don't stop.

She goes through her entire warm-up twice before her muscles feel loose enough to dance. Now, center practice, she tells herself firmly, looking around first. The huge rhododendrons shield her from the path. Feeling self-conscious, she lets the dancing take over. It's different without mirrors. Freeing. She can feel the steps instead of looking at them so carefully for perfection. She goes through her audition dance, once, twice, again. She would have kept going, but ...

"Cassie?"

She stops, mid-*arabesque*, teeters for a moment, then drops down hard on both feet. She whirls around.

"Oh, Matt. You scared me. I was just ... "

"Dancing, yeah. We saw."

He gestures at the tiny blonde girl next to him. Both of them are out of breath from running, shifting back and forth from one foot to another.

"This is Taylor," Matt pants.

"Oh, hi. Nice to meet you."

"So what are you doing in town?"

"You don't want to know." Cassie tries to catch her breath. "Whew! Sorry. Um, I kind of got suspended."

"*You* did?"

"I know. It was stupid. Wanna see why?"

"Okay, sure."

She flashes her belly-button ring.

"Cool," says Taylor. "I always wanted to do that, but I figured I'd pass out or something stupid."

"Well, yeah," agrees Cassie. "It happens."

"So, have you seen Holden?"

"Me? Um, no. Not since Christmas. Why?"

"I don't know. I mean, I don't know what's going on with you two, but I thought you might want to know that his mom's pretty sick. She's in the hospital. Like, really sick. Anyway, he'd probably be glad to see you."

A strange look passes across Cassie's face. "I'll think about it. Listen, I should let you guys get going."

"And you can finish your, um, dance."

"No, I'm done."

She grabs her bag from under the tree.

"Nice to meet you," she calls after them as they jog away slowly, their pace perfectly matched.

A half-hour later, she finds herself outside Holden's house, not sure if she should go in. Then she thinks about the picture he painted of her. She can't go in. She just can't.

She turns around and half-runs, half-jogs back to her house, her sweat-soaked clothes sticking to her like memories.

Behind closed eyes, the whales come again. Outside, the March sky is clear and dark, flecked with shining stars. But inside, in dreams, the whales are circling the pool, circling and circling. Holden is in the water. What is he doing there? He struggles to rise out of sleep, but can't.

He is at the bottom of the pool in his scuba gear, bubbles rising above him. Something is keeping him from moving, his feet clamped firmly to the bottom. He can see the whales – they seem close enough to touch – yet they don't seem to notice him. He can hear them, too, their sonic cries echoing around the pool, around inside his head. It's deafening. It sounds like cries of pain. His hands clamp over his ears, but he can still hear it. He can hear it from inside. He stands at the center of the tank, not knowing what to do. If he moves, for sure they'll see him. They'll come for him, toss him around like prey, like a seal. Or worse, drag him around until he runs out of air, until he can't breathe anymore. Holden is paralyzed at the bottom of the tank.

He sees the splash before the whales do. Looks up. Someone has fallen into the pool! A cloud of dark hair, streaked with silver.

"Mom! Mom! MMMOOOM!"

The whales notice right away. They go to her. They take her.

Holden is woken by his own scream, echoing through the empty attic. Blood-curdling. It only takes a minute for his dad to appear in the stairway.

"What is it? Holden? What's wrong?" In his hand he is holding Holden's old baseball bat.

"Dad ... oh. Sorry. I had a dream, I guess. Sorry, I didn't mean to wake you up."

"Are you okay?"

"Yeah. Forget it, it was nothing."

They stare at each other in the half-light of the moonlit room.

Both of them jump when the phone rings. His dad turns pale.

"I guess I'll get that," he says slowly. "I guess I have to get that."

They both know, of course, before the doctor says anything.

"She's gone," his dad whispers in answer to his question. "She's left us for good."

Holden reaches out. For the first time in years, Holden and his dad embrace. Tears pour down their cheeks.

"I'm sorry, Dad," Holden whispers. "I'm so sorry."

Cassie can't sleep. A dream has jerked her awake, which was bad enough, but when she opened her eyes she couldn't figure out where she was. Now she is lying sandwiched between her ballerina sheets, eyes wide open, adrenaline pumping through her veins. Her hands shake under the covers.

Ridiculous.

She pushes the covers away. She knows herself well enough by now to know when she isn't going to be able to get back to sleep. She gets dressed and sneaks quietly out the front door.

The night is quiet and still, and the air tastes cool on her tongue. She walks down the sidewalk soundlessly, her jacket pulled tightly around her. The moon is huge and luminous, illuminating the carefully cut lawns and newly planted gardens. The breeze smells sweet.

Where is she going?

She wishes she had Max. He wasn't much protection, but at least he was big - not that there is anyone around to bother her. Not at three o'clock in the morning on a cool spring night in this quiet suburb.

She walks and walks until the day starts to break. She walks down to the beach and sits and stares out to sea and thinks about the whale massacre and the baby whale, and thinks, why not? It was all a long time ago. Maybe now, I should help.

Maybe it's what I should do.

Maybe it's what I have to do.

She makes her way slowly home, her back to the sunrise.

All the lights in Holden's house are on. For the second time in twenty-four hours, she stands on the sidewalk outside. Wondering. Something must have happened. She is rooted to the sidewalk.

Time passes.

She can see Holden and his dad passing by the windows.

She's still standing there when they emerge from the front door a few minutes later.

"Cassie?"

"Holden. Hi. I was out walking ... "

"It's six in the morning!"

"I know, but I saw the lights, and I thought ... I wondered ... "

"She died," his father interrupts. "We're on our way to the hospital now."

"Oh. I'm so sorry. Holden? I'm really sorry. Can I do something?"

Holden steps towards her. "No," he says quietly. "I don't think so."

His eyes are red from crying.

They drive away, leaving her standing there on the sidewalk outside the house, empty now, and still lit from within.

Cassie goes inside.

It's probably breaking and entering, but the dawn light feels so strange that she can't stop herself. In the distance, she can hear a dog howling at the sinking moon. She leaves everything as it is, stepping over a pile of newspapers that has been left in the front hall. She goes up the narrow dusty stairs to the attic, sits on the couch and looks around the empty space. It's perfect for dancing, of course. Just like the studio.

Perfect.

Holden won't be home for hours.

Once again, she dances for Holden in his attic gallery. Her bare feet thud against the boards, splinters sinking unnoticed into her callused skin. The *tour en l'air* works perfectly. She does it again and again, until she is dizzy and her feet sting. Until the sun has risen all the way and the howling of the dog gives way to the sounds of traffic and the thud of the newspaper on the front door.

She falls asleep on the couch, her cheek pressed into the raised velvet pattern, worn now to nubs. It is such a luxury, to sleep the exhausted blank sleep of the dreamless. She sleeps and sleeps.

She's still there when Holden comes home. Still there when he leans over and kisses her gently on the forehead, covers her with a blanket. He stares at her, her perfect skin glowing in the morning light, her hair tangled and alive against the dull brown fabric of the couch.

He has brought something back from the hospital – the painting he did for his mom. He props it up on the easel, the girl and the dog behind the veil of leaves.

It's the first thing she sees when she opens her eyes.

"Good morning."

"Hi. Oh. I guess you're wondering why I'm here ... "

"Not really," he admits, his voice cracking from fatigue.

"Oh. The painting ... it's beautiful." She steps back and examines it from all different angles. Her hair swings down and hides her expression.

"So, why are you here?" he asks, finally.

"I just, I don't know. I don't have anywhere ... I mean, I wanted to apologize for before and then I saw

Matt and ... you know, that painting is really good."

"Thanks. My mom was really proud. She said ... she just ... "

"Oh, Holden, I'm so sorry."

She holds out her arms. It's only natural that he comes to her, that he fits himself into her arms, that clothes fly from their bodies. More natural than lifting a bottle to his dry, chapped lips. He drinks deeply from her.

And then she sleeps, again. Dreamless.

Cassie gets home late in the afternoon. Her mother is in the kitchen chopping some questionable-looking vegetables for dinner, while Xav plays on the floor with a filthy soccer ball.

"Where have you been?" asks Xav rudely.

"Out," she answers shortly.

"Now, Cassie. Answer your brother," says her mother reprovingly.

"Okay, I was at Holden's house. His mother died last night. We were having sex. That's where I've been. Okay? Happy, Xav?"

"Moooo-o-m," he whines.

"Honestly, Cassie. You don't have to always be upsetting your brother."

"You've got to be kidding, Mom."

"No, I'm not. I'm tired of us all having to tiptoe around you because something shitty happened in front of you when you were eight. Just how long does it take you to get over that?"

"I don't know, Mom," says Cassie, her voice shaking. "You're the shrink. Why don't you look it up?"

She sleeps for the rest of the day. Dreams that are empty, like white cotton batting. Soft and luxurious.

The funeral is packed with family friends.

"Weird," whispers Holden. "None of them seem to have noticed she was gone for, like, five years."

The eulogy skips over that part, too. The minister drones on about her community involvement, the PTA, scouts. Holden snorts out loud.

Cassie holds his hand tighter. His feet shuffle on the dusty church floor. He pulls away from her, clearing his throat.

The minister is about to say his final prayers when Holden suddenly stands up.

"What are you doing?" she asks, but he doesn't answer.

"Excuse me," he says. "I was wondering if I could say a few words about my mother."

"Oh, certainly, my son. Of course," the minister agrees, graciously.

He stands aside to let Holden take the podium.

"My mother," he starts, his voice breaking, "my mother was a lot of things. People have said some really nice things about her today. And she was all those things. Except you all left one thing out – my mother was an addict. Her addiction is what killed her. She knew that. We knew that. And all of you must have known that. She was gone for five years. Five. No one else has mentioned that, because maybe they think if they do it will somehow make it real. But it was true. It is true. And it is real. And now she is dead. I just think she would want everyone to know that it isn't a secret. She made some mistakes. And I, for one, plan to learn something from them. She was my *mother*. I hope you all learn something, too."

He looks around the congregation, and his eyes settle on his father.

"Sorry, Dad," he mutters.

"Don't be, Holden. It's true."

Someone in the back starts clapping, and it spreads in ripples through the church.

"Honestly," Cassie hears her mother say behind her. "Don't these people know it's gauche to clap in church?"

So Cassie stands up, and claps louder. She claps until her hands sting.

FOURTEEN

"Cassie! Cassie ... " Madame touches her leg. "It's you. It's your turn."

"I can't," Cassie whispers frantically. "I can't."

Her legs are paralyzed, feet frozen to the floor. Everything hurts. Every muscle in her body hurts. "Tell them I'm sick! Tell them something ... "

"Cassie ... "

"Madame, I can't!"

"Get up right now," Madame says firmly. "Now."

Cassie gets up. She goes into the huge studio. The ceilings are so high that looking up makes her dizzy, so she quickly looks away, catching her breath.

At the very end of the room, a row of people sit

behind a table. Other than that, the place is empty. Just the endless row of mirrors reflecting Cassie. A million Cassies, all in a row. She thinks of the other girls in the waiting room, all tall and impossibly lithe, with blonde or brown hair pulled perfectly back in immaculate, shellacked buns. Beside them, she was aware of her own boniness, her wild red hair. Her freckles. Beside them she looks like a clown, she thinks, her heart racing in her chest. Her stomach heaves. I am not going to throw up, she tells herself.

The people at the end of the room are speaking. Something. What are they saying? She can only hear the echo of their words bouncing around her. She squints, but they seem impossibly far away.

" ... you can begin any time you're ready," she makes out.

She nods. She forces herself to nod.

She stands in the center of the cavernous room. Closes her eyes. Waits. She can hear her raspy breathing, her heartbeat. She can feel the sweat beading on her skin, even though the room is cool, almost cold. The people watch politely, waiting.

She takes a deep breath. Nods, to start the music. Wills her muscles to obey. Her eyes are closed. She waits.

When it begins, something like relief floods over her like a cool wash of water. Her feet carry her automatically. She has done this dance a hundred times, a thousand. It's easy, she thinks, relaxing into the movements. Her feet fly across the floor. There is something about the sound of a ballet slipper on a wood floor that reminds her of everything she ever wanted. She dances harder. Extends her legs further. Jumps higher and higher and higher, until her *jetés* lift her above the room, above her nervousness.

Cassie dances. *Echappé. Tour en l'air.*

At the end, the people at the end of the room nod.

"Thank you, Miss Wagner. We'll be in touch."

They turn to one another. "Who's next?"

That's all? Cassie thinks, her blood thundering through her veins. That's it?

She walks stiffly back to the waiting room, and the other girls stare at her, as if they can glean from her face the results. As if they can see something that she doesn't even know.

"But how did it feel?" Holden asks.

"I don't know," Cassie says, twisting the phone cord around her finger, tight, so her fingertip turns purple. "I told you, they didn't say anything."

"But did it feel good to you?"

She shrugs silently.

"Did it?" he repeats.

"I guess. I don't know. I still have to do the other part, the technical part. They come around and do some stuff here, Madame says. I guess we'll have to see."

"Oh."

"What's new with you?"

"Not much. I went on a dive the other day."

"*You* did?" She doesn't bother to hide her surprise.

"Yeah. I was taking this course last year, and I kind of dropped out. But I ran into the guy at a meeting. You know, at AA? And he said he'd take me out again."

"AA? You go to AA? Isn't that for ... "

"Yeah, Cassie. I'm an alcoholic. I've been going for a few months."

"Oh."

"Do you want to hear about the dive? It's the first one I've been on in the actual ocean."

"Okay, tell me. How was it?"

"It was okay. A little spooky. I mean, I looked over my shoulder a lot, I guess. But it was okay." Holden cradles the receiver against his chin, closes his eyes. The dive was beautiful, actually. There was so much life down there on the reef. Not at all what he was expecting. The water was clear, and a current was running gently and he had to concentrate hard on staying in one place. Twice, his mask filled with water and he had to empty it underwater, trying not to panic. But he did it. That counts for a lot. He clears his throat to break the silence.

"Oh," says Cassie. "Sorry. I guess I was thinking about something else. I'm glad the dive went well. I'm glad about AA, I guess ... I just didn't know. Anyway, diving. Wow."

"And I think it's going to help. I'm doing something a little different now, in my paintings? With the light and stuff? I think it sort of works better."

"Good, Holden. That's good. How's your dad?"

"Same. I thought he'd be different, but he's not. He just, like, works all the time."

"How's Matt?"

Holden pauses. "Oh, he's the same."

"Anyway ... "

"Yeah, anyway ... "

"I guess I have to go," Cassie says reluctantly.

"Me, too."

"Night, Holden."

"Night, Cassie."

FIFTEEN

Sina coughs.

"Sorry!" she calls. "Can we do that part again?"

"One more time, Sina," answers Mark. "This is taking too long."

"Okay, here goes."

Sina looks back into the camera. "Every year, seven percent of whales in captivity die. This is high, considering in the wild, only two percent will die in any given year. Yet we keep capturing them, taking them away from what they know, from everything they were born to do. We capture them, and put them in tanks that are not too much bigger than the equivalent of a backyard pool to a person, we take out all the vegetation, the fish, the current. And we expect them to perform in exchange for a dead fish ... "

Five minutes later she's done.

"Perfect!" calls Mark. "Sina, that was great."

Sina smiles. Reluctantly, she steps out of the camera's lights and puts on her glasses.

"You're up, Cassie."

Cassie sighs, shaking his hand off her shoulder. "I know. Okay. Just give me a minute."

She stands motionless under the glaring lights. Mark Mitchell watches, feeling a rush of tenderness. Really, she doesn't look that different than she did nine years ago. A tiny girl, with a huge memory. A memory so big, it has filled almost all the corners inside with fear. Her eyes are huge and luminous as she stares into the camera. Her hair is absolutely rigid in its bun.

Her voice is low and thready. The soundmen motion to each other to adjust the mike. Everyone can see how hard this is for her. No one wants to make her do it again.

"I was playing tag with my friends. It was cold outside, I remember that. We were running around to keep warm. From the tunnels under the Seaquarium, through the windows, you could look up and see the seals and sea lions, the octopus, the fish. You could also see the whales. We were little kids. That's all we wanted to see. During the show, the whales stayed up on the surface. All you could see was white froth and their white bellies moving by, up above."

She pauses.

"But then, something happened."

Her voice cracks. "One of the trainers, she fell in the water. We saw her fall in. It was so surprising that some kids laughed. We didn't know. We didn't understand that the trainers were not supposed to be in the water with the whales. We knew it was cold, though, so I guess we knew it shouldn't be happening. They played with her. The whales."

She stops, tears running down her cheeks. "They dragged her around the pool, underwater. We could see her face. It was something you couldn't stop watching. It was horrible, but you couldn't look away. I remember, at one point, the whale that had her let her go. We could see other things in the water now. Orange life rings. Buckets. She swam past all this stuff, and was at the edge. I remember thinking, thank god, she's okay. I was relieved. I was only eight, after all. I thought it was over. But then, the whales came for her again."

She clears her throat. Blows her nose. The cameraman looks at Mark, raises an eyebrow. Keep going, he motions.

Finally, she starts again:

"This time, they didn't let her go. She drowned. Later, I found out from Mark Mitchell that former trainers at the Seaquarium had been worried that something like this would happen. That people had fallen in before, and the whales had been reluctant to let them go. That once a whale actually pulled a trainer into the water when she put her hand in his mouth during a show. That the trainers quit when their cautions were ignored."

She pauses again, her voice stronger. "All these years, I have been obsessed with my fear of whales. But I realize, now, that my fear is misplaced. I shouldn't be afraid of whales. There's no way I would ever be endangered by a whale in the wild. It's just never happened. The only time the killer whale has lived up to its name is in captivity.

"So I should be afraid of the people who are willing to exploit them. Who are willing to endanger the lives of others to maintain a training technique that so obviously is harmful to the whale's mental health. And probably their physical health. There are other ways.

"I can only hope these places start to use them. I understand that some local aquariums have changed their training styles as a result of this incident and with new research in mind. It's not enough. I don't think it's enough. There are hundreds of whales in captivity around the world. It's not going to stop until people like you stop paying money to see them."

Her voice cracks. "And it's too late for that girl. It's too late. And it's too late for that baby whale that killed herself, committed suicide. Think about that, think about an animal doing something so human as taking her own life. Maybe they're more like us than we know."

She steps out of the light, her shoulders trembling. Mark moves towards her.

"Perfect, Cassie," he says gently. "Thank you."

"I'm never talking about it again," she says, backing away. "Never ask me again."

She runs from the room. Her legs are trembling, but she is still able to run. She runs down the corridor out of the school into the hot June daylight, runs until she gets to the Woods.

She sits down, her back pressed against the tallest tree, facing away from the school, and cries.

That night, Cassie does not dream about whales.

SIXTEEN

"I did? I did? Are you kidding me?" Cassie is practically shouting at Madame.

"Yes, Cassie. You did. I *knew* you would."

"I did?" She screams. "I did? Oh my god! Oh my god!"

She is laughing and crying at the same time. She hugs her teacher.

"Thank you. Thank you!"

"It wasn't me, Cassie. It was all you. You've got the talent and the ambition. You'll go far."

"Thanks, Madame. Thank you."

She runs by Mr. Mitchell in the hall. "I got in!" she calls to him, her voice reverberating around the empty hallway. "I did it!"

"Great!" he calls. "Congratulations!"

She keeps running, out to the Woods. Gravel churns under her feet. Her heart is somersaulting.

She can see Sina, alone under one of the trees facing the school, cigarette in hand.

"Sina! Sina!"

Her friend waves.

"I got in! I did it!"

"You did?" says Sina, a little sadly.

"I did! I'm in!"

Cassie does a *sissonne* in the air.

"Oh," says Sina. "That's ... great. Congratulations."

Cassie's heart falls. "What is it?"

Sina shrugs. "I don't know. I guess now that school's over, I guess I'm kind of overwhelmed. What if there aren't any other parts?" Her eyes squint as though she's trying not to cry. "What if this is all there is?"

"Oh, Sina. You know that's not true."

"I'm sorry. I'm ruining your moment. I'm happy for you. I am. It's just ... I don't know. Maybe I'm jealous?"

"No. You're going to make it. Besides," she adds, "you'll always have somewhere to stay in Toronto if you want to try for stuff in the big city!"

Sina smiles, butting out her cigarette and blowing out the last puff in little rings.

"I know," she says. "I know."

Holden surfaces, disoriented. The sky seems too blue above him, in contrast to the muted blue of the water. "Wow," he says, climbing into the boat. "That was great."

They have been diving in Porlier Pass, in hope of seeing some octopi. The currents are strong, but manageable, and Holden has been practicing a lot with his instructor. It's amazing how much he has accomplished since he joined AA.

"The octopus here are the largest in the world," his instructor promises.

"Wow," Holden says. He can't say anything more, afraid that if he talks about it, he will lose the images. The magnificent images. The beams of sun breaking through the surface. The plants. Everything.

A painting is taking shape in his mind.

That night, in the attic, the painting pours out of his brush. The blue light and shadows, the currents on the surface like swirled glass, the puff of ink. The octopus dwarfs the canvas it is painted on.

He doesn't even hear his dad coming up the stairs.

He doesn't sense him watching over his shoulder.

Finally, he's finished. The brush stops moving. He looks appraisingly at the huge canvas. It's good, he thinks.

"Not bad," he whispers out loud.

"Actually ... " His dad clears his throat. "It's pretty damn amazing."

"Dad?"

"I came up to tell you ... "

"What is it?"

"Cassie called while you were out."

"And?" says Holden impatiently.

"She's going to Toronto."

"Oh." Holden's mood falls. So far away. She's going to leave, and they only really met. His brush moves into the paint again, towards the canvas.

His dad reaches out. Grabs his arm.

"No," he says. "It's perfect now. Don't touch it."

"Really?"

"Really, son."

Holden watches his dad's back recede down the stairway. Notices his stooped shoulders and greying hair. His dad. Maybe he's not so bad, he thinks. Maybe he's okay.

"You can't go to Toronto," Cassie's mother says angrily. "That's silly."

"But Mom, I have to. I mean, I'm going ... "

"I won't allow it."

"You don't have any choice," Cassie says quietly. "I don't know why you want to ruin my life, but I'm not going to let you."

"Ruin your life? I just want to..."

"What, Mother? What do you want to do?"

"Well, to protect you."

"To protect me?" Cassie repeats, stunned. "Protect me from what?"

"From ... everything."

"You can't, Mom. You can't protect me from anything. I have to do this on my own." Through the phone line, she can feel the weight of her mother's sigh. "I'm going," she says defiantly. "I am going to go."

"Yes," she says, "I suppose you are."

Her father comes on the line. "Congratulations, I guess," he says. "We always knew you'd make it."

How could you know, Cassie wants to scream. You never even watched me dance! But she doesn't.

"Thanks, Dad," she says. "I'll be home next week for a few days. To pack and stuff."

"We'll see you then."

"We'll see you," she echoes.

The dial tone severs the connection.

"I'm free," Cassie says to the empty room. Sina's side is clean and deserted. All Cassie's things are packed in boxes. "I'm finally free," she says again.

EPILOGUE

The crowd gasps as the whale explodes from the water and smashes down, spraying them with white water. Once, twice. The sun shines down weakly, but not enough to warm them, and they shiver under their souvenir shirts. A trainer steps out onto the platform and whistles loudly. The crowd watches as the two whales in the pond circle tightly back and stop in front of the jutting, blue deck. The trainer, a girl with a long blonde ponytail, waves at the crowd and then steps into the water with almost no splash. She bobs right back up again and waits for the whale to come up underneath her. She has done this dozens of times and is no longer nervous, is no longer thinking about anything at all. The crowd is huge in front of her, all eyes on her as she waits. Idly, she thinks about the bright colors of their shirts. The cameras all click at once as she is pushed up out of the water on the nose of the gentle giant. Somewhere, she thinks, there are a million pictures of me.

The show is going smoothly. She slides back to her position on the orca's broad back. He races through the water, and she feels the pull of the current and the smoothness of his skin, and the warmth where the sun hits it. She is hot in her wetsuit. She squints at the sky and muses that it is probably almost time to switch to her other outfit, the mesh one that does not make her sweat so profusely. She is not watching as the other whale suddenly rises from the water in a breach.

She doesn't react quickly enough when his body starts falling towards her, falling. She looks up and his body obliterates the sun and then she is between them and hears the horrifying sound of her own bones breaking, all at once or one by one. The cameras snap.

"I don't think this is part of the show," someone says.

Pandemonium breaks out. The girl is pulled from the pool. The whales swim placidly away, leaving her broken body behind.

Maybe they are remembering freedom.

They swim around their enclosure slowly, again and again. Trainers whistle and bang buckets, but the whales continue to swim.

Maybe they are thinking of an ocean without walls.

The girl is lucky. She gets to live. Her bones are patched together by the best doctors, the best surgeons. She is lucky because it is America and the aquarium owners give her a large sum of money. "Hush money," her friends tell her. She doesn't care. She sometimes closes her eyes and dreams and in the night she relives the moment when the whale's body blocked out the sun. That same moment, over and over again.

The incident is talked about only briefly. The aquarium manager is quoted as saying: "It was an accident. A terrible accident."

Too quickly, the story is replaced in the paper by news of a war overseas. A serial killer. People forget about the whales.

The aquarium stays open. Every day, people come in droves and pay their money at the gate. Twenty million people every year. The whales swim round and round, upside down in their "natural" enclosure. Round and round.